AN INSTANT CONFECTION
CULINARY CAT COZY MYSTERY

RUTH HARTZLER

An Instant Confection
Amish Cupcake Cozy Mystery Book 5
Culinary Cat Cozy Mystery
Ruth Hartzler
Copyright © 2020 Ruth Hartzler
All Rights Reserved
ISBN 9781922420794

No part of this book may be reproduced in any form or by any electronic or mechanical means, including information storage and retrieval systems, without written permission from the author, except for the use of brief quotations in a book review.

This is a work of fiction. Any resemblance to any person, living or dead, is purely coincidental. The personal names have been invented by the authors, and any likeness to the name of any person, living or dead, is purely coincidental.

CHAPTER 1

I was glad to get home that day. I was looking forward to the renovation of my new home. I had bought the house from my sister and her husband, Amish farmers who lived on the adjoining farm. I had left the Amish many years ago and had lived in New York for years with my then husband, who, on my fiftieth birthday, announced he was divorcing me.

Octogenarians, Matilda and Eleanor, lived with me in my new house along with their funny little cat, Mr. Crumbles.

Matilda and Eleanor had rather questionable decorating ideas, and they had already decorated the living room to their own taste, which consisted of vibrant and clashing primary colors. My sister had nearly fainted when she had seen it for the first time. I had nearly fainted when I had seen the weapons lining one wall: daggers, swords, clubs, batons, knuckledusters, bows, and shurikens.

They assured me the weapons were only for decoration, but I wasn't so certain.

Still, I wouldn't have to put up with the weapons much longer. They would soon be moved to a part of the house which had been sectioned off to date. There wasn't even a window. For some reason, it had been bricked up years ago by the person from whom my sister and her husband had bought the house and land.

I wondered what was in there. Matilda and Eleanor had assured me they would find a way into that part of the house by the end of the day.

I chuckled to myself as I turned down the dirt lane leading to my house. I passed the fields with Matilda and Eleanor's dreadfully behaved goats. Thankfully, they were not doing anything untoward for once.

I was looking forward to relaxing that night. I got out of my car and walked into the house. Usually, Matilda and Eleanor greeted me. This time, there was no sign of anybody, not even Mr. Crumbles. I walked into the kitchen for a snack.

There was still no sign of anybody. "That's strange," I muttered to myself. Still, I hadn't stayed back at the cupcake store to bake like I usually did, and I was home more than an hour early. Maybe Matilda and Eleanor were out doing something with one of the goats.

This was rather strange. Still, they couldn't be too far away. I pulled out a piece of wet bottomed Shoo-fly pie from the fridge and set it on the table. I cut a slice and put it on a plate.

I figured I should check the adjoining section of the house to see Matilda and Eleanor had gotten into it somehow, but then I chuckled to myself and shook my head. It was all brick. There was no way anybody could get into that section.

I had just finished my pie when I heard a scratching sound. I hoped rats hadn't moved into my house. I looked around and then discovered the scratching sound was coming from under the kitchen sink. I bent down and for the first time noticed a note taped to the door. It read,

Jane, if you're home early, do not let Mr. Crumbles out. It's for his own safety.

I opened the door a crack and peeked in to see an angry cat face.

The kitchen cupboard door flew open, and Mr.

Crumbles flew out. It took me a second or two to realize there had been an ear-splitting explosion. I was certain both of us were airborne for a moment. I landed hard on my back with Mr. Crumbles landing on my face.

"Ugh, argh," I said through a mouthful of cat fur. I struggled to my feet in time to see Mr. Crumbles sprint from the room, every hair standing on end. I was certain my hair was doing the same.

What had happened? I staggered outside.

Matilda and Eleanor appeared around the side of the building. "Jane, whatever happened to you? You look a fright," Eleanor said.

"What happened?" I asked. I knew the two of them had been involved.

They exchanged glances. "We got into the room," Matilda announced proudly.

"Wait! Was that the explosion I heard?"

"Yes, Eleanor used too much explosive."

"I did not!" Eleanor said with indignation. "I wanted to use less, but you insisted."

"I did not insist," Matilda snapped. "You wouldn't let me have an opinion on it. After all, *I* am not the one who is an expert in plastic explosives." She made air quotes at the word, 'expert'.

I clutched my head with both hands. "Exactly - what - happened?" I said slowly through gritted teeth.

Matilda beckoned me to follow her. "We got into the room," she said again. "Come and see, Jane!"

I rolled my eyes and followed them. She was right. They had certainly gotten into that section of the house.

There was a gaping hole in the wall. Rather, there wasn't a wall at all, at least not on one side. Bricks were scattered everywhere. "I'm surprised the roof is still on," I muttered crossly to myself.

Eleanor beamed widely. "I know what I'm doing," she said. "Those plastic explosives are very chemically stable."

I bit my tongue. It was better that I didn't say anything. I carefully picked my way across the bricks and made my way over to where the wall had once been.

"We won't need to cut out a hole for a window in the wall now, will we?" Matilda said brightly. "There isn't a wall."

I remained silent. I didn't trust myself to speak.

I looked into the building. It was simply one rather large room with rafters across the top. It reminded me of a barn construction. "Why on earth would they seal off this section of the house?" I said, more to myself than to anyone.

"They obviously bricked it up from the outside," Matilda said. She pointed to the far wall where the door had been boarded up. "That explains why we weren't able to open that door from the inside of your house."

"I'll have to get someone to replace the wall," I said with a frown. "I hope it doesn't rain first."

I did mental math to figure out how much it would cost me to have a wall replaced. I needed somebody to lay the bricks, and then I'd need to buy windows, maybe even an external door.

I absently walked into the room, but Eleanor caught my arm. "Those floorboards aren't safe, Jane." I followed her gaze, and she was right. There was a narrow hole in the middle of the floor. "Did your explosives do that?"

Eleanor was clearly affronted. "Of course not, Jane. I know what I'm doing with explosives."

I folded my arms over my chest. "And exactly *how* did you come by these skills with explosives?"

"She watches a lot of YouTube videos," Matilda said, as quick as a flash.

Eleanor hurried to agree. She nodded vigorously. "That's right, that's right," she said, still nodding.

I narrowed my eyes. "I'm going to go inside and have a nice cup of meadow tea to soothe my nerves." My breathing was ragged, and I was shaking.

Eleanor pointed to the door with a hammer. "I'm going to open that door." She waved the hammer as she spoke. I hadn't even noticed she was holding a hammer.

"Please try not to do too much more damage." I gingerly picked my way back across the bricks and made my way around the side of the house.

Mr. Crumbles was standing on the porch. His hair had returned to its normal state. "It was Eleanor," I told him. "Come inside and I'll get you some dinner."

I was still speaking when there was another explosion. Once more, I was flung backward, and once more Mr. Crumbles landed on my face.

"Ugh. Err. The door!" I said through a mouthful of cat fur.

CHAPTER 2

For the second time that afternoon, I picked myself up and dusted myself off. Mr. Crumbles ran in the other direction, all his hair standing on end once more.

I was on my way back to Matilda and Eleanor when I heard the sound of a car.

I swung around. To my horror, it was Detective Damon McCloud. I had not seen him since we had kissed the previous week, after which he had been called away on a case. I felt a little awkward seeing him for the first time after we had kissed, and what's more, I was covered in ash and must have looked a fright. A strange smell of motor oil and—what was that? Burned almonds?—hung around me like a cloud.

Damon looked surprised when he saw me. "Jane! What happened?"

Of course, I didn't tell him about the explosives. I very much doubted they were legal, and I didn't want to get Matilda and Eleanor into trouble. "We've been renovating," I said. That, at least, was the truth.

Matilda hurried over to us. "Hello, Detective McCloud. Yes, we have taken down a wall." She was holding a rather large, cast iron mallet. I looked at her with surprise. She was carrying it as though it were a light weight. Where did that woman get her strength? I suspected Eleanor was busily covering up the evidence.

I hurried to say, "Please come inside." I hoped Matilda would give us some alone time, but she hurried after us.

"I haven't seen you for a while, Detective. It's lovely to see you again."

Damon nodded, and rather awkwardly produced a big bunch of flowers from behind his back and handed them to me.

"Oh, they're beautiful." I stuck my nose in the blooms, beautiful pink roses, white roses, and pink mini carnations. I shot Matilda a pointed look, but she simply smiled at me.

I shrugged and walked inside. I put the flowers in a crystal vase and placed it on an oak sideboard which Matilda and Eleanor had painted in rather strange stripes of purple and gold complete with gold glitter. Well, at least it was colorful.

"Has Eleanor finished, um, *renovating*?" I asked Matilda.

"She should be along presently."

Seconds later, Eleanor appeared in the living room. "Where did you come from?" I asked her.

"I told you I'd get that door open," she said. "Now we have internal access to that room."

Damon stood up. "I'd love to see it."

"No!" the three of us said at once.

"I wanted it to be a surprise. We'll do a little more work on it first," I hurriedly added. "Like maybe adding the wall back," I muttered to myself.

"It's strange there was no access to that large room," Matilda said as Eleanor hurried off to brew coffee for everyone.

"A room?" Damon asked. "I thought it was rather a large section with several rooms."

"Yes, wait until you see it," I said. "It's quite big, but it's just one huge room. I have no idea what they used to for."

"I wonder why anybody would have such a big room in a house."

It suddenly occurred to me. "I know! It hasn't always been owned by Amish people, but it was built by an Amish couple. They would have used that room for the meetings."

"What sort of meetings did they have?" Damon asked me.

"Oh, that's what the Amish call church," I told him. "They have meetings every other Sunday in somebody's house. The people in the community take it in turns. Maybe the people who built this house wanted a large room for the meetings."

Damon scratched his head. "So what happens if they have it in a house that doesn't have a big room?"

I shrugged. "That's quite common. The men sit in one room, and the women sit in the other. The ministers walk from one room to another while they're preaching."

"Yes, that would make sense," Matilda said, "but it doesn't explain why it was bricked up."

Damon leaned forward. "It was bricked up, Jane?"

"Yes, haven't you seen it before? There wasn't so much as a window in it. There was an internal

AN INSTANT CONFECTION

door. We thought it was simply bolted from the inside, but when we were in the room, we saw it had been boarded completely on the inside."

Damon appeared to be thinking it over. "How strange. So, somebody boarded up the door and then climbed out the window before bricking up the window."

Eleanor handed everybody a cup of coffee. I thanked her and nodded. "Yes, that seems to have been what happened," I said. "Oh, here comes Mr. Crumbles."

The little gray cat padded back into the room. He looked around as though worried there might be another explosion. Eleanor scooped him up and put him on her knee. He purred loudly. "He looks a little startled," Matilda said.

"It's all the explosions," I said before I caught myself.

Damon quirked one eyebrow. "Explosions?"

"I meant explosive sounds with the hammer and the mallet." I smiled at him. "There was a lot of noise."

Damon simply smiled back. Of course, he wasn't suspicious—who would suspect a pair of wayward octogenarians would use plastic explosives while renovating a house? I shook my head at the thought and then ran my hand across my forehead. Thank goodness my sister's husband wasn't at home or he would have been over here in a flash. I was lucky my sister was back at her cake store training her new young assistant.

Damon stood up. "I have to go."

"So soon?" I said. "You won't stay and share dinner with us?"

"I'd love to, but I've just arrived back in town. I need to go home for a shower and a very long sleep." He reached out and touched my shoulder briefly, sending electric tingles coursing through my arm. "I'll call you tomorrow, Jane."

He nodded to Matilda and Eleanor. I walked him to his car, but unfortunately Matilda and Eleanor followed me. When we were back inside, I said, "I'm surprised Damon hasn't said anything about those weapons on the walls."

"We only have the legal ones hanging there," Matilda said with a big smile. "And we tell everybody they're fake, just for decorations."

"What? You mean they're not fake? And you have *illegal* weapons somewhere else?"

They both looked guilty.

"We'll keep *all* the weapons in the room once

it's fixed," Matilda said. "That's still all right, isn't it, Jane?"

I hurried to reassure her. "Of course, that room is just for you and Eleanor. You and Eleanor can do what you want with it. Only no more explosives, please."

Eleanor frowned deeply. "We won't need any more explosives. All the demolition work has been done. Now, it's just rebuilding."

"Rebuilding," I said with a sigh. "I'll have to call somebody about that tomorrow."

"Your sister and husband will know somebody," Matilda pointed out.

"I'll add that to my renovation list." *My long renovation list*, I added silently. How much was this going to cost?

That night, I found it difficult to sleep. I had an uneasy feeling about the new room we were renovating. Was it simply because they had used explosives to access the room? Or was it because they intended to keep their weapons in there? I had no idea. Whatever the reason, sleep eluded me.

It was a full moon, and the bright light somehow found its way around the edge of my curtains. I tried putting a pillow over my face, but that didn't help me sleep. It was the middle of the night when I finally gave up and decided to have a cup of meadow tea. I always found peppermint soothing.

I was sitting in the kitchen, twirling my teacup around and around when Matilda and Eleanor joined me.

"Would you like some tea?"

They said they would, and both sat down. As I poured some tea into the cups, I asked, "Weren't you able to sleep?"

"I heard you down here," Matilda said.

"Yes, I heard you coming down the stairs," Eleanor agreed. "Are you all right, Jane?"

"I couldn't sleep."

"Where's Mr. Crumbles?" Eleanor asked. "He usually sleeps in my bed."

Just then, we heard a large howl and a strange sound.

Eleanor jumped to her feet. "Mr. Crumbles!"

"It came from that room!" Matilda said. The two of them raced out of the kitchen door, with me hard on their heels. Eleanor flung open the door into the room. There was no electric light in there, but the moon shone brightly through the missing wall.

From a big hole in the floor emerged a form. I gasped. It took me a moment or two to realize it was a cat, a brown striped cat. "A tabby cat!" I exclaimed.

Eleanor edged carefully to the gap by the missing floorboards. "It's Mr. Crumbles!" she exclaimed.

"No, it's a brown tabby cat," I said.

Eleanor disagreed. "It's Mr. Crumbles, and he's covered in various shades of dirt."

I waited until my eyes adjusted. Sure enough, it was Mr. Crumbles, but I had never seen a cat so dirty. Matilda and I carefully made our way over to the hole in the floorboards.

"The floorboards must have given way, and he fell in," Eleanor said, stating the obvious. She looked down, into the hole between the floorboards. "Oh no!"

I edged closer. "What is it?"

Eleanor simply pointed by way of response.

I looked between the floorboards. There, glinting in the moonlight, was a dead body. More than a dead body, it was a skeleton. Embedded in the skull was an ax.

Matilda appeared beside me. "Oh, no, it's a recent murder!"

"A recent murder?" I repeated in disbelief. "That body has been there for years."

Eleanor shook her head. "Not the skeleton. *That* body."

I bent lower, and gasped.

CHAPTER 3

I realized I was holding my phone. I had brought it to use as a flashlight. "I'll call Damon."

Just as I spoke, my hand trembled, and I dropped the phone into the hole in the floorboards. "No!" I wailed. "What am I going to do?"

"We can call the police from one of our phones," Matilda said. "There's no reason to be upset."

"Yes, there is! My phone has fallen onto a body."

"I'll fetch it." Before I could protest, Eleanor jumped nimbly into the gap in the floorboards.

"Eleanor!" Matilda exclaimed.

"I'm not harmed. It was only a short drop," the disembodied voice drifted up to us.

"You're disturbing the evidence." Matilda's tone was scolding. "Whatever were you thinking, Eleanor?"

"I didn't land near one of the bodies, and besides, you've gotta come down here and take a look." Before I could protest, she pushed on. "There's a tunnel in here."

"Aha! That explains everything." Matilda dropped to her knees and shone her flashlight into the hole. "Eleanor, the phone?" She reached in and then produced my phone which she handed it to me.

"Could you get that out of my eyes?" Eleanor said.

"What do you mean?" I asked. "What explains everything? I don't have a clue what you're talking about."

Matilda stood up, dusted off her knees, and turned to me. "Don't you see, Jane? How did somebody murder the more recent victim under the floorboards?"

"How would I know?" I said. "I didn't want to look."

Matilda tut-tutted. "The second victim also

was murdered with an ax, but no Jane, I wasn't commenting on how the victim was dispatched. I meant, how did somebody either murder him here or place his body here? Don't forget, the room has been sealed for decades. You said so yourself, but this victim is quite recent."

I rubbed my temples vigorously. I could feel a headache coming on. "I still don't follow."

Matilda sighed. "You said this part of the building has been walled up for years. Is that right?"

I nodded. "Yes."

"And so, nobody has had access to this room for many years?"

I kept nodding. "That's right."

"And Eleanor had to blast a hole in this room to get access to it. Correct?"

It was beginning to dawn on me. "Oh, I see! Whoever murdered that later victim had to get into this room somehow. Both the murderer *and* the second victim somehow got into this room, but there was no way in until Eleanor dynamited a hole in the side of the building."

"I used plastic explosives," said the voice from the pit.

Matilda nodded her approval. "Yes, that's right,

so there had to be another way in, because both the murderer and the victim found a way in. Unless, of course, the victim was murdered somewhere else, and the body was brought here. Still, that seems unlikely, but I don't want to confuse you."

"It's a bit late for that." I was already thoroughly confused. "So, you said something explains everything?"

"Oh yes. Eleanor said there's a tunnel. The tunnel explains everything. It provides a way in."

"But why would someone tunnel under a building just to murder someone?"

"Murdered *two* people most likely," Matilda said, "although we don't know for certain that the two murders are linked. It seems highly likely though, given it's the same location and the same method of murder. Anyway, let's have a look at this tunnel."

I leaned down and shone my phone into the hole. My phone provided the tiniest amount of light. "Is it an old turnpike tunnel? The old railway tunnels? But aren't we too far from those tunnels?"

"No, no, no. This tunnel is much too small for that," Eleanor called out. "You need to hop in and have a look."

Cold sweat broke out on my forehead. "I'm not going in there! And how would we even get out? It might not be safe."

Matilda tapped my arm. "We'll have to use a ladder. Wait right here, Jane."

While Matilda was away, I stuck my head into the pit again.

"Can you see, Jane?" Eleanor asked me. "I'm shining the flashlight on the tunnel entrance."

"I can't really see from here."

Matilda's arrival with a ladder prevented further conversation. She placed it carefully into the tunnel. "You go down first, Jane."

I made to protest but then realized there was no point. I carefully climbed through the hole in the floorboards, with Matilda right behind me. "Don't go near the bodies," Matilda said. "We can't disturb the evidence."

"Trust me, I don't want to go near any bodies." I pulled a face.

The place under the floorboards was damp, dark, and unpleasant with a foul odour. "What's that white powder?" I asked.

"Quicklime to stop the body smelling and help it decompose faster, I expect," Eleanor said in a matter-of-fact tone. "Let's have a look at this tunnel."

"I'm not going into a tunnel," I protested.

Matilda and Eleanor ignored me. They both edged toward the tunnel and shone their flashlights over it.

"It's a small tunnel!" I exclaimed.

"It's a very strange wall." Eleanor touched the tunnel wall. "It doesn't seem like a regular tunnel wall. It's far too nice. Let's see where it leads."

I gasped. "You can't go in there! What if it collapses on you? What if it narrows?"

"If it narrows, we could send one of the goats in," Eleanor said. "We can buy a security camera and tie it to the goat's collar to film what's ahead."

"Honestly, Eleanor, sometimes you say the most outrageous things," Matilda snapped.

"Well, do you have a better idea?" Eleanor snapped back. "The security cameras are too big for Mr. Crumbles."

Matilda muttered to herself and disappeared into the tunnel. Eleanor stormed off after her. I clutched my phone and hurried after them, not wanting to be left behind.

The tunnel was big enough for a few people to stand side-by-side and for a tall person to stand upright. It was awfully strange. It was cold and dark but was pristine. There was no trash on the ground, and the going was smooth, no bricks over which we could trip.

I wondered why anybody would build such a tunnel. It wasn't as if we were at the coast and pirates could land and hide their treasure in the tunnel. And my sister, Rebecca, had never mentioned a tunnel. I was certain she had no idea it was here.

"What if it collapses on us?" I asked again.

"It's been here for years, and it hasn't collapsed on anybody yet," Matilda called over her shoulder.

Before long, the tunnel narrowed, and Matilda and Eleanor stopped so suddenly that I ran into Matilda's back. Directly ahead of us was a big iron gate covered with mesh. Eleanor's flashlight revealed a huge lock.

"That's to stop critters getting into the section below your house, Jane," Matilda said. "Isn't that good!"

"Err, yes?" I said, wondering what was good about being in a scary, dark tunnel. "Can we go back now?"

"No, we have to follow this tunnel to see where

it leads. Eleanor, how long will it take you to pick that lock?"

"Shush, I'm concentrating," came the reply. Eleanor waved a hairpin at us.

To my surprise, the gate soon opened, and the sisters pressed forward. I am somewhat claustrophobic by nature. I did my best to fight the waves of panic which threatened to overwhelm me again and again. Logically, the tunnel showed no signs of collapsing on us, but fear isn't logical. I hurried to keep up with Matilda and Eleanor, and I fervently wished I had never entered the tunnel.

Finally, the darkness seemed to abate somewhat. I had always thought the expression about seeing a light at the end of the tunnel meant I would see an actual speck of light. Instead, the darkness grew less intense, footstep by footstep. Finally, we rounded the corner, and I did indeed see a tiny light ahead.

"If only we had brought one of the machetes," Eleanor lamented as we approached the exit to the tunnel.

I soon saw the exit was covered with vines and bushes.

The three of us worked hard to make a space

to crawl through, and soon the three of us were out into the dawn.

I gulped the fresh morning air. "Where are we?"

"We're in the woods, of course." Eleanor pointed to a nearby tree.

Matilda rolled her eyes. "I'm sure Jane didn't think it was a beach."

"Why would anybody build that tunnel?" I said, more to myself than to anybody.

"That's a good point, and how would anybody know it was there?" Matilda pointed to the huge rock in front of us. I walked out in front of the rock and looked back toward the entrance to the tunnel. It was certainly well camouflaged, and nobody out hiking would happen across it.

"We had better get back and call the police," I said.

Matilda pointed to the exit. "We'll have to go back through the tunnel because we don't know our way back to your house from here, Jane."

"I'm sure I could find it," I said hopefully.

"No, Jane, the tunnel it is!"

I sighed and followed them back into the cold darkness.

CHAPTER 4

It was all so surreal. I hurried back through the tunnel. It wasn't as bad as the first time, because I knew the length of the tunnel, and I knew where it led—in this case, back to two dead bodies. Still, it also led back to my house.

My house! Would I feel the same about it, knowing there had been two bodies lying beneath? And what if there were more? I shuddered and tried to push the thought from my mind. Surely, it wasn't the work of a serial killer. No, I was simply being fanciful.

Once we were through the iron gate, Matilda pulled it shut, and Eleanor locked it with her hairpin. "There. That's secure. Nobody will get in through that."

"Somebody did," I pointed out. "The murderer."

"I meant nobody would get in without a key."

Moments later, Matilda stopped suddenly, and I nearly ran into her back. "We're almost back at the bodies," she said. "We have to be careful not to disturb the evidence."

"I suspect Mr. Crumbles might have already disturbed plenty of evidence," I pointed out.

Matilda and Eleanor ignored me, but we were already at the ladder. I studiously avoided looking at the bodies and shimmied up the ladder, followed by Matilda and Eleanor. For the first time, I realized they were covered in dust. I assumed I looked a fright as well. No wonder I had mistaken Mr. Crumbles for a tabby cat. And Mr. Crumbles was there, staring at us as if he didn't know who we were. He looked perplexed, turned tail, and ran out of the room.

"I'll call Damon," I said. I was about to swipe and call Damon when Eleanor tapped my shoulder. "We need coffee. Have some coffee before your call."

"No, I'll call him now," I said. "Would you go

ahead and make me some coffee, please? I could really do with some."

As a former Amish person, I had grown up drinking coffee before the sun rose. In all my subsequent years as an *Englischer*, it was a habit that stuck with me. I always needed to get coffee into me as soon as I awoke.

My call to Damon went straight through to his voicemail. I figured he had his phone turned off so he could have a good sleep. I went into the kitchen and told Eleanor and Matilda as much. "And so I'll have to call the police," I concluded.

I did just that. By the time I finished, Eleanor had set a large mug of freshly brewed coffee on the table in front of me. Matilda was busily making herself some coffee soup.

"We had better go and tell Rebecca and Ephraim everything before the police come," I said. "Let's finish our coffee first."

I looked at the time on my watch. I was surprised at how much time had passed. I yawned and stretched and swallowed the last mouthful of my coffee.

Ephraim had already left for work by the time we got to Rebecca's house. Rebecca was in the garden picking some peppermint leaves, no doubt for her meadow tea. She looked up and gasped when she saw us. "*Ach du lieva*! You scared me, for sure and for certain! Whatever happened to you?"

"We had better go inside while I tell you," I said, not wanting to upset my sister too much. "Can we have some *kaffi*?"

Rebecca raised her eyebrows. "*Kaffi* or meadow tea?"

"*Kaffi*," Matilda, Eleanor, and I said in unison.

Rebecca nodded and walked back over to her house. Soon, we were sitting in her plain living room, sipping coffee. "There's no way to break it to you gently, so I'll speak directly," I said. "You know that extra big room at the side of the house?"

Rebecca nodded. "The room that is blocked off? The one you wish to renovate?"

"Yes, that's the one." I shot her a reassuring smile. "Well, yesterday we removed a wall to get into the room, and there were some broken floorboards, but early this morning we heard Mr. Crumbles calling out because he fell in…"

Rebecca interrupted me. "Is he all right?"

"He's fine," I told her. "But the thing is, there were two dead bodies under the floorboards."

Rebecca's hand went to her throat. "Two dead bodies? Are you sure?"

"They are certainly dead," Eleanor said. "Axes are protruding from the bodies' heads."

"Axes?" Rebecca rubbed her temples vigorously. "Oh dear."

"One body looked to be from ten or so years ago, and the other one was quite more recent," Matilda supplied.

Rebecca's jaw was still hanging open. Her hand was suspended halfway to her cup of meadow tea.

"Why didn't you ever try to get into that room?" I asked her.

Rebecca took a moment to recover and shrugged. "Because we have always rented it to tenants, and they had plenty of room in the house. We never really worried about it, you see."

"Didn't Amish people build that house?" I asked her.

She looked up to the ceiling as though trying to recall their names. "Yes, David and Arleta Habegger."

"And do they live in this community?"

"*Jah*. Or rather, they did, but they went to be with *Der Herr* many years ago. The daughter lives in a nearby community. She's a widow and quite elderly."

"What's her name?"

"Linda Lengacher."

I bit my lip. "We should go back to my house and wait for the police to come. Rebecca, I'll probably be late for work today, depending on how long the police take."

"After they finish cross-examining you, you can go to work. Eleanor and I will stay at the house and deal with the police," Matilda said happily.

"Cross-examine me?" I said. "Why, do you think I'll be a suspect?"

Matilda and Eleanor both nodded. "Yes, you own the house," Matilda said.

"But I've only just bought it, and ten years ago I was living in New York."

Matilda shrugged. "I didn't say it was logical to suspect you, but they will have to suspect you, at least on some level."

Eleanor for once agreed with her. "Yes, that's right, you'll be on their list. I will be too and so will Matilda."

I hoped they were exaggerating. "I'll let you know what happens, Rebecca." With that, we walked the short distance back to my house.

I walked directly to the kitchen, this time needing some food. I was on a bit of a caffeine high. I saw my phone on the kitchen table, and it was signaling a missed call from Damon.

"Oh, I should have taken my phone with me," I muttered to myself. To the others, I said, "I'll go into the garden and called Damon back."

I gripped my phone and took it into the garden, thankful that the sisters hadn't followed me. "Damon," I began breathlessly as soon as he answered, "there are two dead bodies under my house!"

"I know. I was informed."

"Are you on your way here?"

He didn't speak for a moment and then said, "I'm afraid not, Jane. I won't be on this case."

I was puzzled. "Why not? Aren't you back at work yet? Or are you on leave?"

Again, the hesitation. "No, it's just that the captain thinks we might be, um, too close for me to be involved in this case."

I was silent, processing his words. Finally, I said, "Oh. I see."

"But I'll call you this afternoon," Damon added. "Are you all right, Jane?"

"It was a terrible shock," I admitted.

"I'm sorry I can't be there for you."

"That's okay."

I made my way back to Matilda and Eleanor. I was sad that Damon wasn't on the case, but then again, I had to admit I was pleased that he was considered too close to me to be involved in the case. That was a good sign, surely. Despite the current situation, little tingles of happiness ran up my spine.

"Will he be here soon?" Matilda said when I walked into the kitchen. She slid a plate of buttered toast across to me.

I thanked her, and said, "No, he's not on the case."

Matilda and Eleanor exchanged glances. Matilda nodded. "Oh yes, because the two of you are romantically involved."

I made to protest. "Oh no, we're not romantically involved. Not exactly."

Matilda and Eleanor both chuckled. Even Mr. Crumbles appeared to be smiling.

CHAPTER 5

After I had a quick shower, I stood on my front porch, one hand on my Adirondack chair, looking for signs of the detectives' car arriving. I didn't have to wait long. A car drove up and stopped outside my house. Two men got out. One wore a furrowed brow and an oversized suit, while the other was much younger and looked like a model. His face seemed familiar, or maybe I was mistaking him for an actor.

I waited on the porch. The younger one broke into a wide smile, showing a row of impossibly white teeth. "Hi, I'm Detective Leo Wright and this is Detective Marvin Collins."

I shot a glance at Detective Collins. He, certainly, was not smiling. His suit hung off him—

maybe he had lost a lot of weight lately. His face was large and covered with deep lines, and his hands were huge. He appeared irritable.

"Hi, I'm Jane Delight," I told them. Before I could say anything else, Detective Collins barked, "Is this your house?"

"Yes," I said, and then looked behind me as Matilda and Eleanor tumbled out the door. "And these are my housemates, Matilda and Eleanor Entwistle."

"Who found the body?" Collins demanded to know.

Eleanor stepped forward. "It was Mr. Crumbles actually, late in the night. Or should I say, in the early hours of the morning."

"Then I need to speak with him too."

Eleanor chuckled. "He's a cat."

Detective Collins's scowl deepened. "Excuse me?"

I thought I had better explain. "Mr. Crumbles is our cat. We heard him in the early hours of the morning. When we went to see what was wrong, we discovered him covered in dirt and emerging from a hole in the room. It was the room we had only just gained access to."

Collins rubbed his forehead. "Show us. But don't go near the evidence."

I walked around the outside of the building. I hesitated at the point where the wall had once been. "I don't know if the floorboards are particularly safe," I told them.

"What happened here?" Detective Wright asked.

"Well, you see, I recently bought this house from my sister and her husband. They live next door." I stopped to point. "They rented out this house for years and when the last tenants left, I bought this house from them. No one had ever been able to gain access to this room."

"So, did you knock this wall down with the bulldozer?" Collins asked. He appeared quite perplexed.

"I believe sledgehammers were used." I tried to sound vague. For good measure, I added, "I don't know much about renovating."

I hoped they weren't going to ask me who did the renovating, but Collins spoke again. "Where are the bodies?" His tone made it sound like an accusation.

"They're in there." I nodded to the hole in the ground. The detectives switched on their flashlights. I hadn't even noticed they were carrying them. They peered into the hole in the floorboards and spoke to each other in low tones.

Eleanor walked over to them. "There's a tunnel under there."

Collins's eyebrows shot up. "A tunnel, you say?

"We didn't disturb any of the evidence," Eleanor hurried to say, "but when we went to see what was wrong with Mr. Crumbles, Jane dropped her phone into the hole by mistake. We went to get her phone, and that's when we saw the bodies. We also saw there was a tunnel."

"The tunnel is of the utmost importance," Matilda added.

Detective Wright stood up and dusted himself off. "What did you say?"

"Like Jane said, this room has been boarded up for years. We think it was built by the Amish people that Jane's sister and husband bought it from. When Jane bought the house, we couldn't get in here at first, because the internal door wouldn't open and there was no external door."

"That's the internal door over there," Eleanor said.

Collins turned around to look. "Go on."

I continued the explanation. "And my sister

said she'd never been in this room. This house came with the farm that my sister and husband live on, but it was on a separate title. This house was always enough for the tenants, so my sister and her husband didn't need to do anything with this room," I said. "They're Amish," I added, "and we only got access to the room yesterday."

"I'm going to have to take statements from you all," Collins said. He looked at his partner. "Detective Wright can take statements from you all, and I'll get the forensics team out here. Wright, go down the ladder and see what you can see."

Detective Wright's smile wavered momentarily, but he climbed down the ladder. He was gone for a full five minutes, and Collins didn't say a word. An uncomfortable silence hung like a shadowy cloud over all of us.

Finally, Wright emerged from the ladder covered in dust. "What's down there?" Collins asked him.

"A skeleton with an ax in its head, a more recent body with an ax in its head, and a tunnel," Matilda supplied before Detective Wright could speak. "Plus plenty of quicklime."

Both detectives looked surprised. Collins shot us a dark look. "If you ladies would kindly go back into your house, we will speak with you in a minute."

"We *are* in our house," Matilda said.

Collins sighed. "If you would be so kind as to go into your living room, we will be with you in a moment."

We skirted back around the outside of the building and went in the front door to the living room.

"Most puzzling," Matilda said. "Why would a perpetrator choose to murder a victim in that particular place?"

"Why would somebody choose to murder *two* victims in that particular place?" Eleanor said.

"Yes, obviously that's what I meant." Matilda nodded slowly. "Jane, we will have to visit this Amish lady."

I was sleep-deprived and over-caffeinated. "What Amish lady?" I said, startled.

"Why, the daughter of the people who built this place, of course," Matilda said.

"The police will question her."

Eleanor nodded. "You're right. We had better get there first."

"Yes, you're right for once, Eleanor. Let's go today."

"Can't we just leave this to the police?" I said hopefully. "It's their job, and they know what they're doing, after all."

A smug look passed over Matilda's face. "So do we. Besides, we're quite bored, aren't we, Eleanor?"

Eleanor was quick to agree. "Yes, we're thoroughly bored. We decided not to enter any more goat shows, and what else do we have in our boring lives apart from the goats? And weapons training?"

I didn't think I had heard her right. "What did you say?"

"She said we have nothing in our boring lives to do apart from looking after the goats and goat training." Matilda's expression shot daggers at Eleanor.

"Then you do the investigating by yourselves. As soon as we give our statements, I'll have to get back to help Rebecca in the shore."

"Not so fast!" Matilda said. "Eleanor and I can't speak Pennsylvania Dutch. You'll need to come with us to speak with the Amish lady."

"I'm sure she speaks English perfectly well," I said with a chuckle.

"No, Jane. You were Amish! She would be more comfortable talking to you."

"Yes, that's right," Eleanor chimed in. "She would be much happier talking to someone who escaped from the Amish."

I was horrified. "I didn't *escape* from the Amish! I just left after my *rumspringa* with the blessing of the bishop and everybody else!"

Matilda patted my knee. "Yes, we know. Eleanor uses the wrong words sometimes."

"I do not!"

Matilda simply rolled her eyes. Before they could get into an argument, Detective Collins walked in. "Detective Wright will be in soon to take your statements one by one. Maybe he could use your kitchen as an interview room?"

I nodded. "That will be fine." I added, "Detective, I haven't told you that my sister and her husband bought this property from the Amish couple who built the houses. They have since passed away, but their daughter lives in another Amish community."

"Thanks. That's most helpful. Make sure you give all those details to Detective Wright." With that, he nodded and disappeared back through the door.

To Matilda and Eleanor, I said, "If you don't mind, I'll go first with the questioning so I can get back to the store."

Matilda appeared affronted. "That won't do! That won't do at all. No Jane, you have to come with us to speak with this Amish lady. I insist." She pursed her lips.

I knew when I was defeated. "Okay, I'll call Rebecca."

Rebecca said she could manage perfectly well with her new young assistant and I could take as much time as I liked. I was rather hoping she'd say I was needed back urgently. When I relayed the information to Matilda and Eleanor, they both beamed at me.

"Well then, it's settled!" Matilda said. "As soon as we're all questioned, we can speak with that Amish lady."

Detective Wright walked in, flashing his teeth at us. "All right. I'm going to take your statements. And ladies, could I ask you not to go into that room for a few days? We'll contact you and tell you when it's clear. It could be several days, maybe even longer."

Matilda shot him a sweet smile. "Whatever you say. We want to be of help."

"Did any of you touch the body?"

"Of course not! We know better than that!" Eleanor said with a frown.

"We watch a lot of crime shows on TV." Matilda continued to smile.

"I'll go first, if that's okay," I said rather too brightly. "Would you like some coffee?" With that, I hurried to the kitchen with Detective Wright hard on my heels.

CHAPTER 6

atilda had wanted to drive, but her driving was scary, to say the least, so I insisted. First, we drove to my sister's cupcake store. I wanted to take some cupcakes to Linda Lengacher, the daughter of the people who had built my house.

Naomi, Rebecca's new young assistant, greeted us. "Rebecca's baking. I'll fetch her."

Rebecca's eyes narrowed with suspicion when she saw us. "I take it you're not coming back to work today, Jane?" She put her hands on her hips.

"Yes. I will if you want me to," I said, hoping she would ask me to stay and Matilda and Eleanor's plan would be thwarted.

"*Nee*, I don't need you back today. Business has

been slow, and Naomi and I are managing quite well by ourselves."

"Are you sure?" I asked hopefully.

"*Jah*. And where are you going?"

"We're going to question Linda Lengacher and ask her about that room," Eleanor said.

Rebecca looked none too pleased. "Shouldn't you leave that to the police?"

I nodded. "Yes, we should."

Matilda stepped forward. "Eleanor wants to speak to Linda, and you shouldn't upset an old lady, should you?"

Eleanor clearly took offense. "Who are you calling old? Speak for yourself!"

"Well then, we had better make a start," I said, to prevent the inevitable argument.

Soon, we were on our way. "Have you ever been to this Amish community before?" Matilda asked me.

"Not as far as I know. If I had, it would have been as a child, but I doubt it. It's too far to drive a horse and a buggy just to go visiting."

Eleanor leaned forward from the back seat. "Let's decide what to ask her."

"Why do we need to decide what to ask her?" Matilda said. "It's obvious, isn't it?"

"If it was obvious, I wouldn't have mentioned it." Eleanor leaned back.

"Lovely weather we're having," I said in an attempt to change the subject. "I hope we don't see the detectives there," I added as an afterthought.

"No, they will have paperwork to process," Matilda said. "I'm sure we will be several hours ahead of them at least."

"I do hope you're right."

Linda Lengacher's address was easy to find. She apparently lived in a *grossmammi haus* behind the house of an Amish couple on a farm. The only place to park was outside the barn, so I parked there, and we got out of the car. An Amish lady came out of the barn and stopped, obviously surprised to see three *Englischers*.

"*Guten mariye*," I began. "I'm Jane Delight, the sister of Rebecca Yoder who is from another Amish community."

The woman's face relaxed. "*Hullo*. I'm Keziah Helmuth."

I hurried to explain our presence. "I live in a house that was built by Linda Lengacher's parents. There's something a bit unusual about the house, so I wanted to speak with Linda. My sister, Rebecca, told me she and her husband bought the farm from David and Arleta Habegger." To clear up any confusion, I added, "Her house and my house are on the same farm." That wasn't so unusual in an Amish community.

Keziah nodded. "Yes, Linda's home at the moment." She pointed over her shoulder to the *grossmammi haus*. "I'm sure she'll be pleased to have visitors." With that, she smiled and walked back inside the barn.

I got the plate of whoopie pie cupcakes out of the car, and the three of us walked over to the *grossmammi haus*. It was an old stone cabin with a wide porch, and the fragrance of the blue buddleia flowers wafted over us on the gentle breeze.

There was no sign of Linda, so I knocked on the door. I immediately heard footsteps shuffling toward the door. The door opened to reveal an Amish lady. She was probably around the same age as Matilda and Eleanor, although she appeared much older.

I at once introduced myself. "I'm Jane Delight. My sister is Rebecca Yoder from another community. These are my housemates, Matilda and Eleanor. I recently bought a house from my sister, Rebecca, and her husband, Ephraim. It used to be on their farm. Apparently, their farm used to be owned by your parents, David and Arleta Habegger."

The woman was listening intently. "Please come in." She opened the door.

I handed her the box of whoopie pie cupcakes. "These are from my sister's cupcake store."

"What did you say your sister's name was again?"

"Rebecca Yoder," I supplied.

She nodded. "I've heard of her. I'm certain I have seen her mentioned in *The Diary*."

"*The Diary*?" Eleanor echoed.

"That's the Amish newspaper in these parts," Matilda said.

"I knew that."

"If you knew that, why did you ask?" Matilda's forehead furrowed into a deep frown.

"I forgot."

"Would you all like some meadow tea?" Linda asked.

"Yes, that would be lovely, *denki*," I said.

We sat in the simple living room. For a *grossmammi haus*, this was quite spacious. There was plenty of cabinet space along the long wall, with shelving units, cabinets, and drawers for storage. Despite the size of the room, it was dark, and heavy, dark blue curtains hung across the small windows. The wall-mounted gas lamps were turned off. A small side table covered with skeins of wool sat next to a large brown armchair. That was clearly Linda's chair, so the three of us sat on the bulky couch opposite.

Linda made a pot of meadow tea and then deposited cups in front of us. She placed some of the whoopie pie cupcakes on a plain white plate. "These are quite unusual. I've never seen anything like them before."

I nodded. "My sister has an Amish cupcake store. She has turned traditional Amish cakes into cupcakes, like these whoopie pie cupcakes, She also makes Shoo-fly pie cupcakes, schnitz pie cupcakes, and Amish Sour Cream Spice cupcakes, to name just a few."

"That seems a sensible idea," Linda said. "You'll have to speak up. I'm a little hard of hearing."

I sipped my meadow tea. After Linda ate half a cupcake, she asked, "Jane, you bought a house my parents built?"

"Yes, my sister and her husband, Ephraim, have a farm. There was another house on the property, on a separate title with five acres. I've bought that one."

"Yes, it is most useful for our goats," Eleanor said.

Linda ignored the goat comment and instead said, "I know the property, but my parents didn't build any houses on it. They bought the farm with the two houses already on it."

"Are you sure?" I asked automatically and then waved my hand at her. "Forgive me, that was a silly thing to ask. Would you happen to know who built it?" I thought it a long stretch that she would know.

"My parents did buy it from the people who built it," she said. "I know that because it had electricity, and my parents had to have the electricity removed from both houses. If you bought the house on the five acres, that would have been the house they used as a *grossmammi haus* for my grandmother. It was far too big for her, of course, but they didn't have anywhere else, and she was happy enough living in it."

"I was wondering why there was such a big room attached to the house," I said. "When my sister and her husband bought the farm, there was a huge room attached to my house, and it was already sealed up. Would you know anything about it?"

Linda nodded rather enthusiastically, so much so, that her glasses fell down onto her nose. She pushed them back up and continued. "Oh yes. It was done for safety reasons, you see."

"Safety reasons?" Matilda echoed. "Whatever do you mean?"

"It wasn't a safe room, given that there was a tunnel under it. It would have been impossible to fill in the tunnel, so my parents simply blocked off the room. They were also worried about critters finding their way into the tunnel, but once the room was blocked off, it was safe."

"So they knew about the tunnel?" I asked.

"Yes. It was made by the people who built the property."

I waited for her to continue. She did not, so I prompted her. "Why would they build a tunnel under a house?"

"You see, they had a petting zoo," she explained. "They had all sorts of animals. They had the tunnel built as an experience. Pirates, I think."

By the time Linda finished talking, my head was spinning. "My sister has no idea about the history of the property. She assumed your parents built the house."

"Maybe the realtor didn't know," Linda said. "And it was so very long ago. I'm surprised your sister hadn't discovered the tunnel before now."

"She's always rented out that house, and it was plenty big enough for the tenants, so she didn't really worry," I explained. "It was only after I bought the house that I wanted to renovate that room. I was awfully puzzled as to why it was fully enclosed like that."

Linda nodded. "*Jah*, my *mudder* and *vadder* boarded up the internal door. There was a big archway to the outside, so they bricked it up. In fact, it wasn't a house to start with. The owners used to live in the other house, and the house you now own was used as a big store and a café."

I was surprised. "There's no sign of that now."

"My parents completely redid it as a *grossmammi haus*. My memory isn't what it used to be, though."

"I see. Thank you for your help. That explains the mystery."

"At least *one* of the mysteries," Matilda muttered.

CHAPTER 7

I'd had a migraine the previous night. It had come on after we had visited Linda, and I had gone to bed in the late afternoon. I suffered from visual migraines. They started out with small flashing zigzags of many bright colors spreading their way across my vision and causing blind spots. I rarely got an actual bad headache with them, but I did have head pressure, and worse, migraines left me shaken for the next few days. I'd had them all my life.

I awoke feeling much better. I brewed coffee, fed Mr. Crumbles, and soon Matilda and Eleanor joined me for breakfast.

"How's your migraine?" Matilda asked.

"It's gone, thankfully, but I still feel a little light-headed."

"In that case, we should visit Wanda today and see what she knows about the victims," she added.

I held up both hands, palms outward, in front of me as a gesture of disagreement. "No. Wanda's daughter, Waneta, wouldn't have heard anything by now. It could take weeks to identify the skeleton."

Matilda drummed her fingers on the table. "On the contrary, the skeleton would have been a missing person for years, and no doubt, the second victim is also a missing person. Given the fact that the two are obviously connected in some way, I don't think it will take long to identify them."

"I think you're being a little optimistic." I sipped my coffee. "Besides, I have to put in a full day's work at the cupcake store today."

Matilda clapped her hands once. "Then that's settled. We will visit Wanda after work. That will give her daughter a full day filing in the coroner's office to come up with some information."

"But what if they don't know anything by this afternoon?" I said.

Eleanor piped up. "No harm, no foul." I noticed for the first time she was wearing a pale pink bathrobe covered with images of gray goats. Jumbo size hair rollers covered her head.

"How do you like my new bathrobe?" Eleanor asked, no doubt as she saw me staring at it.

"It's, um, most unusual," I said honestly.

"Yes, I got it online. It was a bargain."

Matilda muttered something, but thankfully Eleanor did not appear to hear.

"All right then, it's settled. After the store closes, I'll drive home, and the three of us can visit Wanda to see if Waneta has any information."

The day passed in an uneventful manner. We had a rush of customers at lunchtime and then not so many in the afternoon. Rebecca's new assistant, Naomi, was coming along nicely. About fifteen minutes before closing, Rebecca walked over to me. "Why don't you go now, Jane? It doesn't seem as though there will be many more customers today, and you keep looking at your watch."

"Thanks, Rebecca. I have plans with Matilda and Eleanor."

"You're going to drop by Wanda's house."

I was shocked. "How did you know?"

Rebecca chuckled. "You're fairly predictable, Jane."

Matilda and Eleanor were waiting for me on

the front porch. I didn't even have time to turn off the engine before they sprinted down the stairs and jumped in the car. "Isn't this exciting!" Eleanor said after placing a wet bottom Shoe-fly pie on the back seat.

"It is indeed," said Matilda. "What are you waiting for? Let's go, Jane."

Wanda was usually working on her vegetable garden when we arrived, but this time she was nowhere to be seen. Her buggy horse wasn't tied outside, so the three of us walked to the house. I raised my hand to knock when the front door flew open. "Right on time!" Wanda exclaimed. "*Wie gehts?*"

"We're good, thanks. Am I really so predictable?" I added with a chuckle.

"*Jah*," Wanda said. "Come in. I have dinner ready."

"Dinner?"

"I was expecting you," she said simply.

We all thanked her. She showed us to an old oak dining table that sat just outside the door to the kitchen. Freshly baked bread, pretzels to be eaten with ice cream for dessert, and various relishes sat on the table. Amish people often dropped by unannounced at dinnertime, and it was the done thing to feed everybody.

Wanda accepted my offer for help. The table was soon laden under creamy mashed potatoes, creamed celery, John Cope's corn, and chow chow. I could see Matilda and Eleanor were desperate to find out about the victims, but they knew it would be impolite to ask before they had eaten some of the meal.

After we had eaten the main meal, I helped Wanda clear the table. She indicated I should take an Amish Peanut Butter Pie to the table, and she followed me with ice cream.

Wanda chuckled. "You must all want to hear what Waneta discovered about the victims."

Matilda was the first to speak. "Yes! Did she find out anything?"

Wanda nodded. "She did indeed. They were actually both members of the Johnson Gang."

I had never heard of the Johnson Gang, but both Matilda and Eleanor gasped. "The Johnson Gang from California?" Eleanor asked.

"*Jah*. They robbed banks in California and then came here and robbed banks closer to their home. The men in the gang were from these parts, you know."

Matilda and Eleanor exchanged glances. "We didn't know," they said in unison.

"I've never heard of the Johnson Gang," I said.

Matilda was the one who answered me. "They were an infamous gang from just over ten or so years ago. You would have been living in New York at the time, Jane, but I'm surprised you didn't hear about it on the news."

"I probably did, but I wouldn't have taken much notice," I said. "I generally don't watch the news because it's usually bad news. I prefer good news."

Matilda and Eleanor looked at me as though I had gone mad. Matilda gave a little shrug and pushed on. "They robbed one of the big California banks of fifty million dollars before coming back to Pennsylvania to rob other banks of lesser amounts, but still substantial amounts."

I was shocked. "Did they get away with it?"

"Obviously not, since two of them were murdered under your house," Matilda said.

I was silent for a moment, processing the information. "And how many were in the gang?"

"I do believe there were five," Eleanor said, looking at her sister for confirmation.

Matilda nodded. "That's right. I'm certain

there were five. And Wanda, two of those five victims were found under Jane's house?"

"*Jah*, that's right," Wanda said.

"Well, that's all very strange." I scratched my head and then dipped a pretzel in some ice cream. Since no one else was speaking and had turned to their desserts, I added, "That explains how the two deaths are related but why ten years apart?"

"Waneta said four of them were released from prison only recently."

Matilda set down her spoon with a thud. "Aha! Then that explains it. They got out of prison recently and murdered the more recent victim who had obviously squealed on the others."

"Squealed?" I asked, followed quickly by, "Oh, he was the snitch?"

"We don't know, but it's a good possibility," Matilda said.

"Was all the stolen money accounted for?" I asked Wanda.

"I don't know anything about that," she said. "Waneta just told me that they were members of a famous gang and told me the name and a few other small particulars."

"Please thank Waneta for us," I said. "That's very helpful."

As we sat in Wanda's living room after dinner, drinking meadow tea, Wanda invited us to play Dutch Blitz, a card game popular among the Amish.

"Jane, I can't believe we don't play this much at home," Matilda said after five minutes. "This is a lot of fun."

I forced a smile. I simply wanted to go home and call Damon to have a nice chat. Still, it was good company, and it brought me back to the days of my youth.

Nevertheless, my mind kept turning to the bank robbers. Why were two of them murdered under my house?

When it was time to leave, we thanked Wanda. I was half out the door when I heard Matilda say to Wanda, "Did Waneta happen to mention anything else?"

I turned back. Wanda hesitated for a moment and then said, "Nothing you don't already know. Only that one of the bank robbers used to own the house Jane now owns."

CHAPTER 8

"But, what, what?" I sputtered. "We saw the lady yesterday whose parents built that house. The lady told us that her parents bought it from the people who had the petting zoo."

Wanda's mouth fell open. "Oh, I'm sorry. I thought you knew?" I continued to look blank, so she pushed on. "I'm surprised Rebecca and Ephraim don't know. No, the house was built by Martin Marks's *familye*. They sold it to the petting zoo people. The petting zoo people didn't build it."

"But Linda, the Amish lady, said that the petting zoo people built it as a store and café, and her parents converted it."

Wanda shook her head. "*Nee*, the people with

the petting zoo converted it to a store and café after they bought it from Martin Marks's *familye*."

"And Martin Marks was one of the bank robbers?" Matilda asked.

"*Jah*." Wanda stopped to scratch her chin. "This was all some time ago, and I'm much older than Rebecca and Ephraim. They obviously didn't know the history of the farm when they bought it."

"But wouldn't they have heard about an infamous bank robber?" Eleanor said, followed quickly by, "Of course, your sister is Amish, Jane. She and her husband don't watch the news."

Wanda chuckled. "But news does travel very fast in our community. This was a long time ago. From what I remember, the parents were embarrassed about their son. He wasn't raised in that house, mind you. In fact, I don't know if he ever lived in the house, but after his parents died, he inherited it."

I was still somewhat puzzled. "So, did the man who became the bank robber sell it directly to the petting zoo people?"

"Yes, I believe he did. I can't be certain, mind you."

We walked back to my car and wasted no time discussing the turn of events.

"But it doesn't make any sense," I protested. "Do we know the identity of the skeleton yet? If Martin Marks is the skeleton, then he obviously couldn't have been alive to sell it to the petting zoo people."

"Obviously, he was murdered after the petting zoo people took over," Eleanor said.

Matilda grunted. "No, course not, Eleanor. Don't you see? He was *murdered*. The petting zoo people would have noticed a skeleton at the beginning of their tunnel!"

"Then this is terribly puzzling," I said. "He went missing ages ago, and nobody looked under my house."

We were silent for a moment. Matilda finally broke the silence. "Maybe somebody lured him to that place to murder him, knowing nobody would ever find him, after the petting zoo was sold and it was boarded up. We'll have to find that exact date and see if it fits in with the estimated date of his death," Matilda said.

"That's a good idea." I thought about it and then added, "I need to write all this down. It's making my head spin."

"You not getting the migraine back again?" Eleanor's voice was filled with concern.

"I certainly hope not. No, I don't think so. So, what do we do from here?"

"We research the two victims, for a start," Matilda said. "We don't know if the skeleton *is* Martin Marks. And it seems whoever murdered the first victim also murdered the second victim. Possibly, the murderer was confident due to the fact nobody had ever discovered the first body. That would have to narrow it down to the members of the gang who have recently been released from prison. The timing is rather obvious."

"But isn't it *too* obvious?" I asked. "I'm sure the murderer doesn't want to go straight back to jail. Those men would know the police would suspect them."

"Then our next move will be on our computers," Eleanor said. "We don't have to worry about dinner since Wanda kindly provided it, so we can spend a few hours on our computers turning up as much evidence as we can."

It didn't take long to get home, and I was surprised to see a car outside of my house. When I got out of my car, the moonlight illuminated the figure of Detective Damon McCloud.

He hurried over to me. "Jane, are you all right?"

I was taken aback. "Yes, why wouldn't I be?"

"I've called many times and left texts, but there was no response."

"That's strange. I didn't turn off my phone or turn down the volume." I reached into my purse and pulled out my phone. "Oh, my battery is flat! I must've forgotten to charge it last night when I had a migraine."

"Let's all go inside." Damon cast his eyes over the landscape. I thought his behavior rather strange but kept my opinions to myself.

When we were inside, Matilda asked, "Would you like some coffee, Damon? Or some hot meadow tea?"

"Coffee would be nice, thank you." Damon sat there looking stern until Matilda returned with meadow tea for the three of us and coffee for Damon. She deposited a plate of red velvet cupcakes directly in front of him.

"Where's my cupcake?" Eleanor asked.

"We have just had a big meal," Matilda protested.

Eleanor pouted. "But if I see a cake, I have to eat it."

Matilda rolled her eyes and went back into the kitchen, this time returning with an oversized plate of assorted cupcakes. She put it on the coffee table with a thud and then said, "Are those enough for you?"

Eleanor smiled widely. "Yes, thank you."

I came straight to the point. "What's going on, Damon?"

"I don't want to worry you," he began, but Matilda interrupted him.

"Beginning a sentence like that is a guaranteed way to worry somebody."

Damon uttered a rueful laugh. "We discovered the identity of the victims."

I almost said we already knew they were bank robbers, but Matilda wisely hurried to speak first. "Really? And who could it be?"

"The first victim was a bank robber by the name of Craig Williams, and the second victim was a bank robber from the same gang by the name of Todd Johnson." To me, he said, "Have you ever heard of the Johnson Gang?"

"Only recently," I said. That, at least, was the truth.

Damon gave a half nod and pushed on. "Martin Marks was in the same gang. His parents built this very house, Jane. He inherited it when they died. I don't think he ever lived here. He sold it to some other people who sold to an Amish family who, in turn, sold it to Rebecca and Ephraim."

"Are you certain?" I said.

Damon seemed surprised by my question. "Yes, why?"

I thought carefully before answering. "I don't think Rebecca knows that. She told me Amish people built the house. I assume the bank robber's parents weren't Amish?"

Damon chuckled. "Certainly not, and I am aware Rebecca didn't know. When you weren't home, I spoke to Rebecca and Ephraim. They told me you were visiting with an Amish lady."

We all nodded. I hoped Damon would not make the connection.

"Yes, we just had dinner there," Matilda said. "Damon, if the bank robber, Craig Williams, was murdered after his bank robber friend sold the house, how did he end up buried here? Surely, the body was deposited there after Martin Marks no longer owned the house."

"Yes, exactly," Damon said. "I admit it *is* a bit of a puzzle."

I held up one hand. "Wait a moment. Damon, how do you know all this? You're not on the case."

He flushed beet red. "No, but Detective Wright has kept me appraised of events."

I bit my lip.

"And there's more, isn't there?" Matilda asked.

Damon nodded. "The three remaining members of the gang were released from prison only recently."

"So, it looks as though one of them is the murderer," I said, "given that Todd wasn't murdered until the other three were released from prison."

"It looks that way," Damon said, "but Detective Wright hasn't given me any indication as to whether there are other suspects. It's not wise to jump to conclusions."

Matilda readily agreed. "Quite so, quite so."

"And why do you think Jane is in danger?" Eleanor asked.

Damon gave a little start. "What makes you think I think that?"

"It's written all over your face," Eleanor said.

Damon appeared surprised by her words. "I'm concerned about the three of you. The bank robbers were active for some years before they were finally apprehended. Detective Wright told me the amount of ten million dollars is still outstanding."

"When you say 'still outstanding', do you mean they've still got ten million dollars?" I asked him.

He nodded. "Yes, a possible scenario is that Martin Marks hid the money somewhere around here."

I was horrified. "In my house?"

"Somewhere on your five acres." Damon made a sweeping motion with his hand.

"Maybe under the floorboards or elsewhere in Jane's house," Eleanor added.

"Then those bank robbers will come here and try to murder us all in our sleep!" I could hear my voice rise to a high pitch, but I was unable to prevent it. I needed to feel safe in my own home, and right now, I felt anything but. I jumped to my feet.

Damon at once crossed over and put his arm around me. "We don't know for certain that you're in any danger, Jane. It's just that I'm concerned for you." He looked at Matilda and Eleanor and added, "And both of you as well."

Eleanor picked up Mr. Crumbles. "And Mr. Crumbles. If only I had continued with his attack training!"

"What are we to do?" I asked.

"Is Rebecca's apartment still leased? You could go back there."

"No, Aaron Alexander still has the lease," I said. "Is Rebecca safe?"

"Certainly. I think all the neighbors, including your sister and her husband, are safe," Damon said. "These people aren't serial killers. They are after the ten million dollars, and they might suspect it's hidden here. Jane, maybe you all should stay somewhere else for a while."

"I want to stay here," I protested. "I'll buy some security cameras tomorrow."

"We can take care of ourselves," Matilda said. "Eleanor and I used to do martial arts."

Damon opened his mouth to speak but quickly shut it. It was clear he had thought the better of voicing his opinion, and just as well.

"Jane, I really don't like you staying here until this matter is resolved. Any of you staying here," he amended.

"If Jane wants to stay, I'm sure we'll all be perfectly safe," Matilda said.

"I'll ask Detective Wright if he would agree to a patrol car passing by once or twice a day."

"Don't worry about that," I said. I thought of

all the movies where patrol cars passed by a few times a day, and those movies never had good endings. I shuddered.

That night, I lay in bed, jumping at every little sound. Maybe I *should* think about staying somewhere else. Maybe the three of us and Mr. Crumbles could go to a hotel. Still, we had to return to look after the goats, but that would be safer sleeping in a dark house at night.

I had considered my house to be my own little sanctuary, but I had never suspected that two murder victims were lying under the house all this time.

CHAPTER 9

I awoke the next morning before dawn as usual and staggered down the stairs in search of coffee. To my surprise, Eleanor was already in the kitchen. She looked hot and flushed. "Good morning, Jane," she said more brightly than anyone should for such a time of day. She set a cup of coffee in front of me.

Mr. Crumbles was sitting on one of the kitchen chairs licking his paws and washing his face. His empty food bowl sat on the floor near Eleanor's feet. Clearly, he had enjoyed an early breakfast.

"Thank you." I reached for my coffee and sipped some. After I had a few more mouthfuls, I asked, "Why are you up so early?"

"I was concerned about the hole in the wall,"

she said. "We don't want goats getting in there and falling through the floorboards. I've started to make a fence, but I still have more work to do. I didn't want to wake up you and Matilda by making banging sounds."

"Thanks," I said. I finished my coffee and poured myself a second cup. "Did you mention goats getting into my house? Why would goats get into my house? They have their own field. Don't tell me they have escaped?"

Eleanor chuckled. "Oh no! Of course not. It's just…" Her voice trailed away, and she appeared to be deciding what she should say next. After a long interval, she spoke. "You know Billy?"

"Yes, of course I do. The one who attacked the bishop?"

Instead of looking embarrassed, Eleanor nodded enthusiastically. "Yes, he's quite vicious! I'm going to let him into the field around the house. No murderers will be able to get in here without having to face off with Billy. And he's very good at sneaking up on people to attack them."

I sighed and wiped my hand over my forehead. "But Eleanor, Billy will attack us too! How will we ever get from the house to the car? And if we try to drive the car out through the gate, Billy might escape."

Eleanor did not appear the least perturbed. "No, I thought of all that. You don't need to worry. I've thought of everything."

Matilda stomped into the room, looking decidedly grumpy. "What on earth are you talking about, Eleanor?" she asked as she poured herself a cup of coffee.

"I've decided to let Billy into the field around the house after I fence across the missing part of the wall. I was just explaining it all to Jane. Billy is very good at sneaking up on people to attack them."

I expected Matilda to say it was a crazy idea, but to my utter surprise, she agreed. "You know, that's not one of your silliest schemes after all, Eleanor. I think the idea has some merit."

A wide smile broke out on Eleanor's face. "Jane was just saying that she can't park her car in front of her house, because when she drives through the gate, Billy might escape. Before you came in, I was about to suggest to Jane that she parks her car outside of the gate."

Had they both gone mad? "But Eleanor, how

will we get from our house to the gate without Billy attacking us?" I protested.

Eleanor continued to smile. "Billy won't attack you if you feed him hay. All we have to do is walk to the gate and back while feeding him hay. Jane, you can keep some hay in your trunk, so that when you stop at the gate, you just have to take out some hay and walk into the house holding it. And we can keep some hay in something on the porch that Billy can't break into, and we can take some of it when we need to leave the field around the house."

My head was spinning. "No, I think it's a crazy idea," I said honestly, "and it will be a lot of trouble walking to the gate and back with hay."

"But it's not far," Matilda said. "And wouldn't you sleep better if you knew Billy was outside the house waiting to attack an intruder?"

I thought about it. "Yes, you're right." They were indeed right—I would sleep much better knowing the vicious goat, Billy, was outside. I certainly didn't want to have another sleepless night like the one before, and I didn't want to leave my home. Billy, indeed, seemed to be the solution, no matter that it was a strange solution.

A knock on the door startled us all. "Who could that be?" Eleanor said.

Without responding, Matilda marched to the door. Moments later, she showed Damon into the kitchen.

"Damon!" I said in surprise. "I wasn't expecting you. And so early in the morning!"

A slow red flush traveled up Damon's face. "I'm sorry, Jane, but you've always said you rise early. I was worried about you all night, so I've brought a security system."

It was then I noticed the box he was carrying. "Oh no, I don't mind at all," I said. "It's good to see you. Would you like some coffee?"

Damon said he would and sat at the table opposite me. Matilda poured him some coffee and set the cup in front of him. "Would you like some *kaffi* soup too?" she asked him.

Damon looked puzzled. "What's that?"

"Just say no," I said with a chuckle. "Some Amish people like coffee soup. You make coffee with cream and pour it into a bowl then drop in stale bits of bread. Matilda likes it."

"I'll pass on that one, thanks," Damon said with a chuckle. "This coffee will do me just fine."

"We could do bacon and eggs," Eleanor said. "Or, to be Amish along with the *kaffi* soup—

although I know you're not having any, Damon—we have some scrapple."

Damon rubbed his stomach. "Bacon and eggs sound good to me. Only I don't want to put you to any trouble."

"It's no trouble at all." I stood to prepare the food.

Matilda waved me back down. "No, you two just sit there and chat while I make the food. What's this about a security system, Damon? And did you happen to have one lying around? Or where did you get one so early in the morning?"

Once more, Damon looked embarrassed. "I have friends in the security business," he said. "I was able to get this late last night." He pulled out some little white cameras. "I'll install these for you, and I can set up the app on your phone, Jane. That way, you can see who's coming and going in real time. I can set it to alert for people, and it has a playback facility."

"Will a goat set it off?" Eleanor said. "Does it have a goat setting?"

"A goat setting?" Damon repeated. He shot me a look.

I rubbed my eyes. "Do you remember Billy, that vicious goat?"

"I sure do," Damon said with feeling.

Matilda hurried to explain. "Eleanor is currently building a fence across the missing wall, and then she is going to shut the front gate and release Billy into the field around the house. He likes to sneak up on people and attack them."

"I'm going to park my car outside the front gate, so next time you come here, park your car outside the front gate too." I would have said more, but Damon interrupted me.

"But how will I get inside the gate, because Billy will attack me?"

"Hay is the answer," Eleanor said. "I did suggest Jane keep hay in her trunk, but now I see I will need to place some sort of waterproof container outside the gate with hay in it. You're perfectly safe from Billy if you have hay. He's a slow eater and likes to nibble, so anyone is safe walking from the gate to the house if they have a large handful of hay. I will also put a goat-proof container of hay on the front porch. Everyone will be safe as long as they remember to hold hay when they're in the field surrounding the house."

Damon stared at me as if waiting for me to object. Instead, I said, "I thought it was a very strange scheme at first, but I must admit I will sleep better at night knowing Billy is loose."

"Surely, you'd sleep better at night if you weren't staying here, and *I* would sleep better at night not worrying about you." He quickly amended his statement. "Not worrying about the three of you."

"I wouldn't worry," I said with a laugh. "Billy is vicious. He'll attack anybody."

"But have you considered that it might be more than one person?" Damon said.

I hadn't considered that, and I said so. "Do you mean the three surviving gang members might be in it together?"

"Undoubtedly," Damon said. "And I doubt Billy could attack three people at once."

"Oh yes, he could!" Eleanor said. "I have every confidence in Billy."

A text sound emanated from Damon's phone. He read it and then gasped.

CHAPTER 10

*D*amon stood up. "I'm sorry, Jane, I have to go. I'll install these when I get back."

"You have to work on a Saturday?" Matilda asked.

"I'm afraid crime doesn't run Monday to Friday." Damon's smile was rueful.

"It doesn't have anything to do with this case, does it?" I asked.

Damon hurried to reassure me. "No, it's another case. I'll see you later, Jane."

For a moment, I thought he was going to kiss me, but then he looked at the sisters and left the room.

"I didn't even realize it was a Saturday," I said. "I don't have to work today."

Eleanor tut-tutted. "But you always work on a Saturday morning."

I shook my head. "Didn't I tell you? Rebecca and Naomi are going to a barn raising." I didn't mention that I had offered to mind the store with the help of Matilda and Eleanor, but Rebecca had quickly declined and said it wouldn't hurt the store to stay closed for the day.

Eleanor rubbed her hands together with glee. "Excellent! That means we can spend the day investigating."

"What type of investigating?" I asked, at once suspicious. Mr. Crumbles leaped into my lap and purred loudly. He held his neck forward so I could tickle him under his chin.

"I was up late, researching on my laptop," Matilda told me. "I discovered that one of the bank robbers is married, and I found she works in a hair salon."

I held both my hands in front of me in a gesture of protest. "There's no way I'm letting her cut or color my hair!"

Matilda and Eleanor exchanged glances. It dawned on me that this had been part of their plan. I crossed my arms over my chest for further emphasis.

Matilda stared at me, but I didn't look away. Finally, she sighed dramatically. "All right then, if you insist. Eleanor can have a cut and color."

I expected Eleanor to shriek with protest, but she appeared quite pleased. "That would be wonderful. I wanted a change in style. My current style is so hard to keep up." She pointed to the abundance of jumbo rollers in her hair.

"Then are we going to let Eleanor go by herself?" I asked Matilda.

"No, I'll see if I can book us both in for a deep conditioning treatment while Eleanor is there. I'm going to call them at nine when they open and see if we can book in for today."

"Surely, they will be booked ages in advance," I said.

Matilda simply shrugged. "Online it says that Martin Marks's wife is working in the salon all day, so that means we can go to his house and speak with him."

My day was going from bad to worse. "Speak with him?" I echoed, alarmed. "Whatever are we going to say? Hello, Mr. Marks, could you tell us if you murdered Craig Williams and Todd Johnson?"

"Of course not, Jane," Eleanor said in reasonable times. "Late last night, Matilda and I decided we would collect for the Amish. Surely there is a current cause we could collect for?"

"Yes, the barn raising," I said. "A family's barn burned down, and they need the money."

Matilda beamed. "Excellent! We can safely question him while his wife's away."

I shook my head. "He will probably slam the door in our faces! Why would he give us the time of day? At best, he might make a small donation before shutting the door in our faces. What can you hope to discover from that?"

"At the very least, we can get a sense of the man," Matilda said, "and maybe even peek inside his house. At least it's an opening."

I resigned myself to my inevitable fate. "Okay, so when do we do this?"

"As soon as we confirm that his wife will be at the hair salon today," Matilda told me. "What a shame Damon had to leave so suddenly. I suppose I will have to eat his bacon and eggs."

After breakfast, I helped Eleanor build a temporary fence across the area where the wall had been. "If only the police would finish with this soon," I lamented. "Then I could find a builder to repair the floorboards here." I wondered if I ever would be able to use that room, given what had happened to it.

We had just finished putting up a rudimentary fence to replace the missing wall and prevent Billy from getting into the room, when Matilda hurried around the side of the building. "Good news! Martin Marks's wife, Daphne May, *is* in the salon today. I booked you in for this afternoon, Eleanor, and Jane, I booked both of us in for deep conditioning treatments."

I was at once suspicious. "That's a red flag, surely," I said. "Don't you think it strange that there's no waiting on bookings? Maybe, Daphne May is a really bad hairstylist, and that's why we could begin so easily."

"Her skill level is of no importance to us," Matilda said. "What's more important is that Eleanor gets the opportunity to question her."

Eleanor looked quite put out. "Well, it's important to me."

"You'll be all right," Matilda said with a dismissive wave of her hand. "What's the worst that could happen? Your hair grows quickly, and you could always color it again if she does a bad job."

Eleanor pouted. "We won't have time to organize Billy."

"You can do it later this afternoon." With that, Matilda hurried around the side of the house.

It wasn't long before I was driving to Martin Marks's house. I found it easily, thanks to Eleanor's directions.

The house was an unremarkable white, wooden house with no front fence. It was set back off the road and partially obscured by trees. I drove past his house a little and parked. "We should pretend to collect from other people first in case he's suspicious and chats with his neighbors after we leave," Eleanor said.

Matilda disagreed. "What nonsense! Why would he be suspicious? We look like a couple of old ladies, and Jane looks like a boring, middle-aged woman."

"Thanks a lot!" I said.

Matilda simply walked off in the direction of Marks's house. I hurried after her before I realized I had left the collection can in the car. I passed Matilda who said, "Maybe he's around the back," to Eleanor.

A man ran up the side of the house. "Have you seen a dog?" he asked urgently. "My dog is missing.

I just found my back door open." He sounded quite panicked. "She's black and white, and fluffy."

"If we see her come, we'll come and get you," Matilda said. The man ran back down behind his house without saying another word.

Matilda grabbed my arm. "That's it!" she said. "That's our way in! We have to find his dog. Quick, Jane, back to the car."

The two sisters ran to the car. I took off after them, but I couldn't catch them. How did these elderly ladies learn to run so fast? I was a little over half their age but did not have their speed.

"Now what?" I asked when I jumped in the car, panting for breath.

Matilda waved both arms at me. "We have to find that dog, of course. Off you go, Jane!"

"His house backed onto the woods, so obviously the dog's there," I said.

"Nothing is obvious, Jane," Matilda said. "Drive around the street slowly, and we will look in everyone's yard."

I drove slowly, thinking it was a wild goose chase. We drove up and down the street with no sign of the dog. "Do it again," Eleanor said, but Matilda disagreed.

"Turn left," she said. I turned left and

continued driving. Finally, Matilda decided we should go back to Marks's street.

"I said that the first time," Eleanor complained.

I suddenly slammed on the brakes. "That's a black and white dog!" The dog was walking along, sniffing in somebody's garden. "We don't want to startle him," I said.

Before I knew it, Eleanor was out of the car and sprinting across the road, while slipping something from her pocket. The dog walked over to her and she slipped a piece of rope around her neck. The next thing I knew, she and the dog were in the back seat of my car. "What did you give that dog?" I asked her.

"Some of Mr. Crumbles' treats," she said. "I always keep them in my pocket."

I didn't even bother to ask about the rope around the dog's neck. Matilda and Eleanor seemed to keep several unexpected items on their person.

"Well, don't just sit there, Jane," Matilda admonished me. "Take the dog back to Martin Marks."

When I brought the car to a stop outside Martin Marks's house, he was standing on his front

AN INSTANT CONFECTION

lawn, frantically looking this way and that. I got out of the car. "Is this your dog?" I asked him.

He ran over to the dog. "Fang!" he said with tears in his eyes. "I thought I'd never see you again." He was all choked up. I expected him to burst into sobs at any moment. "May I offer you ladies a reward?"

"No, but a cup of hot tea would be nice," Matilda said. "It would settle my elderly sister, who is *much* older than I am. She's the one who caught your dog, and she has a heart condition. A nice cup of tea would help."

Marks at once looked alarmed. "Would you like me to call 911?"

"No, I have just had my pills, so a cup of tea would be lovely please," Eleanor said in feeble tones.

He beckoned us inside. "Yes, of course! It's the least I could do! Please come inside. I bought some cake this morning."

He hugged his dog and patted her, and then let her inside the house. For the first time I noticed he was limping.

The house was terribly messy and smelled strongly of dog. I was taken aback. A pile of discarded clothes sat in the hallway alongside a long-dead potted plant. I wondered why they hadn't thrown it out ages ago. From the entrance hall, we turned right into a spacious, yet chaotic living room.

Martin asked us to sit. "Would you like tea or coffee?"

"Coffee for me, please," I said, whereas the sisters said they would both like tea.

"Please put plenty of sugar in it for my poor elderly sister," Matilda said. Eleanor continued to glare at her and clutched her chest.

Martin presently returned with a tray of coffee mugs and a large plate of chocolate chip cookies. He left the room and returned with a large chocolate cake. The whole time, Fang stuck to him like glue. Martin sat on the couch opposite us, and Fang sat beside him.

Martin rubbed his knee vigorously and winced. "I can't believe you were able to catch Fang and put her in the car. Fang doesn't like people, and she has been known to bite."

"I love all animals," Eleanor said. "I have a vicious goat."

Martin leaned forward. "Excuse me? I didn't quite catch what you said."

"Just ignore her," Matilda said. "Dementia, you

understand. She has no idea what she's saying, but she is good with animals."

Eleanor clenched her teeth.

"I can't thank you enough. I haven't seen Fang for ages, and we were reunited only recently. I missed her, you see. I had to go away for a while because of, err, work, but my wife took good care of her. She baked those cookies too."

"They're absolutely delicious," I said, and they were. I pictured his wife around my age, a kindly woman who must have been distraught that her husband was away in prison. Still, it was clear she wasn't one for housework. A print of a fruit bowl hung at an angle over the fireplace, and the mantelpiece was entirely cluttered with all manner of ceramic frogs.

"Does your wife collect frogs?" I asked him.

A pained look passed over his face. "Yes, I'm afraid so. Daphne May is an avid collector." He nodded to an old oak china cabinet in the corner of the room. It too was packed with frog ornaments. Large frog ornaments sat on the floor.

"It's good to have a hobby," Matilda said brightly.

The room was entirely depressing. It was dark, and the curtains were drawn, but I expect Martin was worried the police might look inside. It smelled damp and unpleasant, and I couldn't wait to get out of there.

Matilda was still speaking. "It's good to have a dog, what with the serial killer around."

Martin jerked a little. "A serial killer?" he repeated.

Matilda nodded. "Haven't you heard? Two bodies were found not far from here, and they were both killed in the same manner. The first victim was murdered over ten years ago, and the second victim only recently. This means the serial killer has started murdering again, and goodness only knows how many bodies have yet to be discovered!" Her hand flew to her throat.

Martin's expression remained impassive. I suspected he would be good at poker. "I did see something about it on the news. I wouldn't worry about it."

I could see Matilda wasn't going to push it. "I do hope you're right. Maybe I should get a dog like Fang, and then I'd feel safe."

Martin smiled. "She's a good dog."

It was just as I'd thought. This was a complete waste of time—that is, unless Matilda or Eleanor had somehow gained some insight.

CHAPTER 11

We all stood in an inauspicious alley next to a dumpster, looking at the sign above Daphne May's hair salon.

Curl Up and Dye.

"You didn't tell me the name," I said to Eleanor.

She beamed at me. "Clever, isn't it?"

"I hope dear old Daphne May doesn't give me an old fashioned style," Eleanor complained.

"Who are you calling old?" Matilda said. "I'd guess her husband is twenty or thirty years younger than you are."

"Not that you'd know it." Eleanor ran a hand up and down herself. "He looks *so* much older than I do."

Matilda rolled her eyes.

I cast a nervous look around me. "We had better get inside before we get mugged."

As soon as I opened the door of the salon, loud music assaulted my ears. An overpowering smell of incense or some type of sickly sweet substance that I could not identify hung heavily on the air.

A woman about my age looked up and smiled. "Right on time. Which lady is having the color and cut?"

Eleanor put up her hand.

"Come with me," she said. "You two, please take a seat, and I'll be with you in a moment."

I looked at the woman, thinking she was just as I had imagined Daphne May: a kindly soul, rather rotund, with large rosy cheeks and a sensible haircut. The poor woman—how she managed to keep the household going with her husband away in jail all these years was beyond me. No doubt, she could have retired by now, but instead she had to keep working. No wonder her house wasn't the most pristine house I had ever seen. My heart went out to her. I certainly hoped her husband wasn't the murderer, for her sake.

She placed a black cape around Eleanor's neck and fastened it.

"I want a change," Eleanor told her. "I'm tired of my same old style."

The woman beamed at her. "Well, you've come to the right place. I'll be back in a moment. I'll attend to your friends now."

She gestured me over to the basin first. After a quick shampoo of my hair, she towel dried it and then put a nice smelling substance in it. After that, she wrapped my hair in Saran wrap and told me to sit next to Eleanor. She placed a wall-mounted hairdryer over my head.

I was pleased I was sitting next to Eleanor so I could hear Eleanor's conversation with Daphne May. Still, I had to sit there and wait until she repeated the process on Matilda. To my delight, after Matilda's hair was treated, she was seated on the other side of Eleanor. That meant Eleanor was between us, and we could hear everything that was said.

"Are you both happy to stay there until Daphne May is finished with your friend?"

I was taken aback. "You're not Daphne May?"

She chuckled. "No. She's late. She had to run some errands this morning. Oh, here she comes now."

I swung around, and it was all I could do not to

gasp. Daphne May looked like a weightlifter. I had never seen such muscles on a woman before. What's more, razor blades hung from her earrings and from her nose. She had more studs than Eleanor's favorite studded chair.

Daphne May was wearing tattered black leather and an angry expression. Her head was completely shaven, and she had apparently shaven her eyebrows as well, because all I could see were two black lines drawn halfway to the top of her head, giving her a perpetually startled appearance. Her lipstick was blood red.

She walked over to Eleanor and grunted. "What do you want?" she grunted. Her tone seemed harsh, angry somehow.

"I want a change," Eleanor said.

"Did you bring a photograph or do you have any idea of the type of change you would like?"

"No, you have a free hand."

Matilda and I exchanged glances. I knew Eleanor shouldn't have said that.

"Are you certain?"

Eleanor nodded happily. "Surprise me!"

For the first time, a wide smile broke out on the woman's face. "Oh. it's lovely to have a client like you," she gasped. "I can tell you, it's made my day. Why, you wouldn't believe the stress of having all these clients coming in, wanting the same boring hairstyle time after time." She clamped a meaty hand down on Eleanor's shoulder.

No wonder that poor woman was so tense and angry, I figured, given what her husband's illegal activities.

Daphne May wheeled over a black plastic tray and from it retrieved a pair of rather large scissors. She chopped away at Eleanor's hair. I had to admit, it did give her a more modern appearance. "Do you mind if I do a little bit of shaving?"

Eleanor waved her left hand at her. "Shave away!" She quickly added, "But I don't want hair like yours, as nice at it as it is. I still want *some* hair."

Daphne May chuckled. "Of course, of course. Leave it to me. Now, are you sure that I can shave parts of your head?"

I shot Eleanor a warning look, and so did Matilda, but she was impervious to our hints. In no time at all, Eleanor's hair was transformed into a mohawk. I wondered why Eleanor didn't protest, because even from the front, I'm sure she could see the style.

"Now I will put some nice color on it for you. Do you have any preferences?"

"No, do whatever you like," Eleanor said. "It's so nice to find a stylist as adventurous as you."

The woman clasped her hands in delight. "I can tell you, you've made my day. I'll just pop to the back room and mix your color."

I looked at Matilda and raised my eyebrows. She shook her head slightly. I knew that was a signal that I shouldn't tell Eleanor she had a mohawk. I mean, couldn't she see it for herself? Apparently not, as she sat there in silence until Daphne May returned.

Daphne May applied the color. I couldn't see what color it was, because it all went on white, despite the fact she told Eleanor she had used two different colors in her hair.

"My new hair is going to surprise everybody," Eleanor said.

Daphne May readily agreed. "It sure will! You will be the envy of the whole town."

"On second thoughts, maybe I shouldn't stand out in this town at a time like this. After all, I'm over eighty, and I'm a bit scared about the recent crimes."

Daphne May took a step backward. "What?

You're over eighty? No way! You've got to be kidding me."

Eleanor's smile widened. "No, it's true! That's why I think I should blend in. The new serial killer in town might be more inclined to kill me if I stand out."

Daphne May stopped coloring and stared into the mirror at Eleanor. "Serial killer? Is there a serial killer?"

"Oh, haven't you heard? The police found two dead bodies murdered in exactly the same manner. It's all over the news! They think they were murdered ten years apart. That means there was a serial killer ten years ago, and he's just started murdering again!" Her hands flew to her mouth in a gesture of mock terror. "Why, none of us are safe in our beds at night!"

Daphne May looked shocked. She didn't speak for a moment, and when she started coloring again, her hands were trembling. In fact, she didn't speak again until the other lady took me to wash out my treatment.

When Eleanor's color was finished, Daphne May said, "Now, I'll just leave that there to process." She put a wall-mounted hairdryer over Eleanor's head and vanished into the back room.

The other lady, who had never disclosed her name, came out. She offered us magazines to read and asked us if we would like a bottle of water. We all accepted the magazines but declined the water.

None of us dared speak, so we sat there for a further twenty minutes thumbing through magazines. Daphne May certainly had a reaction when Eleanor mentioned the murders. Did she suspect her husband? Or was her reaction simply based on the fact that two of her husband's gang members were the victims and that her husband was a suspect? There was no way to tell.

CHAPTER 12

*D*aphne May did not return until the other, still nameless, lady washed Eleanor's hair. She wrapped a towel around her hair and sat her in front of the mirror. It was only then that Daphne May entered the room. She had appeared to have recovered her composure. She took off the towel and reached for a hairdryer.

As the seconds passed, I became increasingly surprised. Eleanor not only was sporting a mohawk, but the shock of hair on top was a vivid, fluorescent green, and the remaining hair on both sides was bright orange.

I was struck speechless with horror. I kept staring at Eleanor, waiting for some sort of reaction, but she simply sat there. Daphne May fussed with her hair for what seemed an age, fluffing the top higher and higher. Finally, she applied a lot of product and finished it off with hairspray. Then she grabbed a mirror and showed Eleanor what it looked like from behind. "What do you think?" she asked triumphantly.

"It's unique," Eleanor said. "I couldn't have imagined it would turn out so well."

Daphne beamed from ear to ear. "I love it when clients give me a free hand. It really suits you."

"Yes, the bright green and the orange suit her complexion perfectly," Matilda said with a straight face.

I didn't trust myself to speak.

When it was time to pay, we all handed over cash. Matilda and Eleanor had warned me not to use a credit card, and we had all given false names and addresses.

"Would you like to book in for another appointment now?" Daphne May asked Eleanor.

Eleanor smiled and nodded and supplied a false name and phone number.

I couldn't get out of there fast enough. When we finally reached the safety of my car, I turned to the sisters. "Why are you both taking it so well?"

"Taking what well?" Eleanor asked.

"Your hair, of course!" Had she completely taken leave of her senses?

"Oh, it's nothing to worry about. It will grow back and meanwhile, I can use one of my wigs."

That was news to me. "You have wigs?"

"Of course we do."

I shook my head. "It was very good of you to go through all that for the sake of questioning Daphne May."

I drove away slowly, still shaken by the sight of Eleanor's hair. "So, what did you think of her?" I asked them.

"I think she is quite a good head colorist," Eleanor said. "I know it's a little unusual, but I do think it suits me."

"Honestly, Eleanor! Jane was asking about the case."

I chuckled. "Yes, the case. Did you see her reaction when we mentioned the bodies?"

Matilda and Eleanor both said that they did. "I was thinking it over while I was looking at countless magazines," I told them. "It's hard to know whether that reaction was due to the fact that her husband is a suspect or whether it is due to the fact that she knows he did it."

"I don't think he did it, because he was nice to his dog," Eleanor said. "He obviously loves dogs."

"Maybe he does love dogs, but maybe he doesn't love people," Matilda pointed out.

Eleanor agreed with her. "Yes, you might be right. Still, I hope it's not him, because if he goes back to jail, his dog will miss him. That poor dog."

Eleanor continued to talk about the dog while I—and I assumed, Matilda—tuned out. I was looking forward to lying on the couch with my feet up and maybe catching some TV.

However, as soon as we walked onto the porch, Matilda and Eleanor stood stock-still. "Somebody's been here," Eleanor said.

"How do you know?" I was completely mystified.

"Your front door has been forced open." This time it was Matilda who spoke.

The front door looked perfectly normal to me, but when I walked over to it, I could see it was slightly ajar. Matilda went to walk through it, but I laid my hand on her arm. "What if somebody is still inside? Wait out here, and I'll call Damon."

"Eleanor, you stay with Jane so we don't disturb the evidence. I'll have a look around." With that, Matilda took a pair of nunchaku out of her

AN INSTANT CONFECTION

purse and handed her purse to Eleanor, before slipping on some gloves. Eleanor's expression was deadpan. Could this day get any stranger?

Matilda slipped inside, and I wasted no time calling Damon. This time, he answered at once. "Matilda, Eleanor, and I have been out all day. We've just arrived home and we're on my front porch. The front door has been forced open."

"I'll send uniformed officers out there right away, and I'll be there as soon as I can," Damon said. "And Jane, whatever you do, don't go inside. All of you go back and sit in your car. Lock the doors, and drive off at the first sign of anyone." With that, he hung up, leaving me staring at the phone.

I looked at Eleanor. "What are we going to do? We can't go to the car without Matilda."

It was another few minutes before Matilda rejoined us. "There's nobody around, and they were very careful not to disturb anything," she said. "Don't mention to Damon or anyone that I slipped inside."

"Damon told us to go and sit in the car until uniformed officers arrive."

Matilda nodded and took her purse from Eleanor. "Then that's what we will have to do."

She slipped off her gloves and dropped those along with the nunchaku back in her purse.

The uniformed officers didn't take at all long to arrive. I expect they were nearby when the call came. They both stared at Eleanor's hair, their jaws hanging open.

After we introduced ourselves, I said, "When we came home, the door was ajar."

"Are you sure you locked it before you left?" the shorter one said.

"I'm absolutely positive," I told him. "We're quite on edge, what with the bodies being found under the house and all."

The officers exchanged glances. One of them went to look at the door. "Yes, it has been forcibly opened."

The two officers stood with their heads bent over for a full minute. Finally, the taller one stood up. "Ladies, please return to your car, and we'll take a look inside."

It was another five minutes before the officers came back to the porch, and the three of us piled out of the car.

"It looks like whoever was here is well gone," the taller officer said. "We will get a fingerprint team out here, but would you please go through

AN INSTANT CONFECTION

the house, touching as little as possible, and tell us if anything is missing? We need to know if it was a robbery, although usually robbers make a mess, and the house is quite neat inside."

"Is Mr. Crumbles all right?" Eleanor asked him.

"Yes," Matilda said, and then hurriedly added, "I saw him at a window."

The shorter officer smiled. "You mean the gray cat? Yes, he's very friendly."

I went straight to my bedroom. My jewelry was there, and my laptop was sitting on my nightstand. I walked downstairs and looked around. Eleanor and Matilda presently joined me. We all agreed that nothing had been stolen.

The taller officer handed me his card. "Call if you discover that anything's missing."

"But isn't this to do with the murders?" Matilda said. "The bank robbers. One of them used to own this house. What if he thinks that the missing millions are in this house, maybe buried under a floorboard or in a secret passageway?"

Both officers frowned deeply. One was about to speak when Detective Collins appeared at the door.

"Please come in," I said.

He came in, followed by Detective Wright. They both gasped when they saw Eleanor's hair but did not comment.

The two officers quickly brought them up to speed, and Detective Collins just as quickly dismissed them.

"Yes, we will get a fingerprint team out here," he said. "Do it in a hurry, Wright."

Detective Wright went away to make the call.

"Have you ladies touched anything in this room?" Collins asked us.

We all shook our heads. "I only checked in my bedroom." I raised my eyebrows at the other two.

"We did the same," they said in unison.

He nodded. "Good. Would you please go somewhere for a few hours until the fingerprint squad's has finished." He said it as an order, not a question.

"Sure, we can go to my sister's house next door. I saw her buggy horse in the field when we drove home. She must be back from the barn raising. When will we know we can return to my house?"

"I'll call you," he said. "Ladies, thank you for your cooperation."

"It's the money, isn't it?" Eleanor said. "The

bank robbers have come here to look for the missing millions."

"Oh, so you know about that, do you?"

We all nodded. "Detective Collins, do you think we're in any danger?"

He appeared to be considering my question. "It would be good if you could all stay somewhere else until this case is solved, to be honest," he said. "It does seem unlikely this was a simple burglary, especially as nothing was taken, and I don't believe you disturbed the perpetrator. No, I think somebody was having a good look through your house. Is there anywhere on the property where something could be hidden, maybe an old well? Do you have an old building such as a barn?"

I shook my head. "No, there's nothing like that," I told him. "Only the tunnel."

"I really don't feel good about you helpless ladies living here," Collins added.

"Helpless!" Eleanor said, but Matilda swiftly elbowed her in the ribs.

"Yes, helpless old ladies, that's what we are," she said. "Helpless."

"So, have you decided to stay somewhere else for a while?"

"How long before you solve the case?" I asked him.

He shrugged. "How long is a piece of string? We might solve it tomorrow, or we might solve it in a week. Maybe we won't solve it for a month. Some cases are never solved."

"I can't leave my own home for a month," I said. "or forever," I added in low tones.

"Then would you agree to leave for just a week? If the perpetrator wants to come back, then you won't be here, and you'll be safe."

"I'm not going to leave my home vacant just so the murderer can come and search my house freely," I said indignantly.

"It's all right, I have a vicious goat," Eleanor told him proudly. "An attack goat. And what's more, it comes naturally to him. He hasn't even been trained!"

The detective looked at her as though she were mad. "Excuse me?"

"I have a dangerous stealth goat." Eleanor pointed out to the field. "His name is Billy, and he's already attacked the bishop."

The detective's jaw fell open. Eleanor pushed on. "This morning, Jane and I built a fence across the missing wall to the room where the bodies were found. This afternoon, we are going to shut the gate and let Billy into the small field around the house. He will attack anyone who comes in here. That way, we can all sleep easy in our beds at night. And you don't need to worry, Detective Collins, because Billy sneaks up on people before he attacks them."

The detective just stood there, his jaw working up and down. It seemed Eleanor thought she should add more for clarity. "But just in case you wonder how we will get from the house to the car, you needn't worry, because we have a system figured out." She shot him a look of pure triumph.

The detective shook his head, turned around, and walked out of the door.

CHAPTER 13

As soon as the detectives left, Eleanor grabbed my arm. "Quick, let's investigate Scott Simmons, one of the bank robbers. He sells used cars. I saw it on his Facebook."

Matilda shook her head. "Only two of us should go, in case it gets around that three women have been asking questions. Eleanor, you stay behind to place the hay outside the gate and on the porch."

I thought Eleanor would object, but to my surprise, she readily agreed. "The system will be in place by the time you get home, so make sure you park outside the gate and feed Billy the hay."

The car dealership was on our side of town. Even as we approached, I thought it looked rather seedy. It was hard to find somewhere to park, so we had to drive around for some time. I ended up parking some distance away, but Matilda said that was good to prevent the man from seeing our license plates.

We walked along until we reached the dealership and then made a show of looking at cars. It was a while before anybody came out. The man who approached us was clearly not Scott Simmons. "Can I help you ladies?" he asked. "Are you looking for anything in particular?"

"I'm looking for a car for my aunt," I said, nodding to Matilda.

"What sort of car would you like?"

Matilda shrugged. "I'll just have a look at the cars you've got here." Her tone was entirely dismissive.

The man got the hint. I expect he thought we were lookers and not buyers. When he was out of earshot, Matilda tapped my arm. "That's Scott Simmons over there."

Scott Simmons currently had a customer, and the two men were looking under the hood of a white car. We kept looking at cars until the customer walked away. Matilda hurried over and I hurried after her.

AN INSTANT CONFECTION

Scott Simmons saw us coming and broke into a smile. He ignored Matilda, who was in front of me, and addressed me. "Hello, can I help you?"

"My aunt wants to buy a car," I said, nodding to Matilda.

"And what sort of car would she like?"

Matilda waved one hand in front of his face. "I'm standing right here!"

He chuckled. "How cute. And do you have a license to drive, dear?" He raised his voice and leaned forward. I expect he thought Matilda was awfully hard of hearing.

I wouldn't have been surprised if steam came out of Matilda's ears. As it was, her face turned beet red. "Yes, I have a Class A license, and I have done advanced and defensive driver training, I'll have you know, young man."

He chuckled as though Matilda was making it all up. Again he addressed me. "And what sort of car is she looking for?"

I turned to Matilda. "What sort of car are you looking for?"

"A red one," she said. "What about this red one here?"

He seemed taken aback. "Isn't it a little large and powerful for you?" he yelled in her ear.

"Surely, you would need something more sedate?"

I was surprised Matilda managed to keep her temper. "What else do you have in that price range?" she asked him, her tone reasonable. "I don't want a large car, you understand. I want a car about this length to make parking easier."

"Look at this lovely white car next to it," he yelled. "It's only a foot or so longer than the other car."

"But that model doesn't have a backup camera, does it?"

The man looked shocked, as if wondering how Matilda would know that. "No, but it's absolutely no trouble for us to install one for you."

"And how much is it to install one?" Matilda asked him.

"I'd have to go to the office and look at up."

"Ballpark?"

He shrugged. "Maybe a thousand dollars."

"A thousand dollars!" Matilda exclaimed. "You'd have to do a bit better than that. And we don't have a trade-in, so do you give a discount for no trade-in?"

The man shook his head. "All these cars are very reasonably priced, so we don't have any discounts at all, and we have a no haggle policy. You'll be wanting finance, I assume?"

Matilda shook her head. "Cash."

The man looked at me. "Cash?"

I nodded.

"I'm rather partial to this red car here," Matilda said.

"Have you looked at many other cars?" Again, the raised voice.

"Yes, we've spent the day looking at cars, and I haven't seen one I like as much as this one. I'd like to keep looking, but my niece insisted I buy one in a hurry. She is tired of being dragged around to look at cars, you see."

"It *is* rather irritating," I said, trying to sound genuine.

"Would your aunt like to take it for a test drive?" Scott asked me.

"Yes, that's a good idea," Matilda said. "I shouldn't buy it without taking it for a test drive."

"Then please come into the office. I'll have to take a copy of your license."

We walked into the spacious office, and he indicated we should sit on a comfortable green couch. "Help yourself to tea, coffee, and water," he yelled at Matilda, indicating a tiny kitchen.

Matilda handed him her license, and he disappeared into a back room. I wiggled my eyebrows at Matilda.

"What is it, *Prudence*?" she said after an interval.

"He's got your license," I whispered. "He knows your real name and where you live."

"That's only a problem if he's the murderer," she whispered back. "Besides, the address on my license is still my old address, the apartment above Rebecca's store."

"You haven't changed your address yet?"

She looked entirely smug. "No, I thought it might come in handy. And I was right."

"I must admit, I'm relieved."

Scott Simmons was another five minutes or so. I hoped he wasn't putting a call to his accomplices, but then again, Matilda had given a false address, and there was nothing to connect her with my address.

He came out and then said to me, "Are you coming with us?"

I nodded. "If that's all right?"

"Yes, certainly. Please come with me."

As we walked down the steps, I saw that somebody had brought the car to the bottom of the steps. He bent down to yell in Matilda's ear. "Can you drive shift?"

"Yes," was all she said.

Matilda got in the driver's seat, and Scott climbed into the passenger seat. He looked over at me in the back seat. "My name is Scott Simmons."

I was glad I hadn't called him Scott before he had actually introduced himself—that would have been entirely too suspicious.

Matilda answered him. "You obviously know my name is Matilda Entwistle, and this is my niece, Prudence Entwistle."

He turned around to shake my hand. "Nice to meet you, Mrs. Entwistle."

"Nice to meet you too," I said. He spent a few minutes explaining the workings of the car at the top of his lungs to Matilda, before giving her directions to a quiet country road out of town. Clearly, he didn't trust her driving.

Matilda started quite sedately, and I saw the man's shoulders relax. I could tell he had assumed Matilda was going to be a terrible driver. After an interval, he yelled, "You're quite a good driver."

"I do have a car, but I've just given it to Prudence's nephew, Horatio," she said. "It will be

Horatio's first car. It's too slow for me. I want a fast car in case I need to make a quick getaway."

The man gasped. I expect using the word 'getaway' was a bit too close to home. "What, whatever do you mean?" he sputtered.

"I live alone," she said. "What if the serial killer comes for me? I need a fast car to get away."

"Serial killer?" The man seemed entirely confused.

"Yes, the serial killer who's been on the news lately. Haven't you heard? There's a serial killer in these parts."

"No, I don't think I've heard," he said. He looked over at me for confirmation. "Is this true?"

"Yes, of course. Everyone's terrified. They found two bodies, and they think there could be more."

"Maybe ten or twenty bodies," Matilda said.

I leaned forward between the two seats. "Now, don't worry yourself, Aunt. You know how the news often exaggerates. There might not be more than two bodies, after all."

"And where are these bodies?" he asked.

Matilda shrugged. "I don't know, but I think they were found in a house on a little farm. The newspaper said they were under the floorboards, but the strange thing is that one was murdered about ten years ago, and the other one was murdered only recently. That means it's a serial killer, and he's just started killing again."

When he didn't respond, she added, "You know, I saw something like that on one of those English sleuth TV shows the other day. What's it called, Prudence?"

"Agatha Christie?"

"No, it wasn't an Agatha Christie movie."

"*Father Brown?*"

"No, that wasn't it."

"*Midsomer Murders?*"

"Yes, that was it. I think so, anyway. I find that show so confusing at times. The reason he stopped killing was because his mother found out he'd been killing people. He stopped and didn't kill for another nine years, but when his mother died, he started killing again. Do you think maybe that's the case now?"

He still remained silent, so I leaned forward once more to address him. "Haven't you seen it on the news?"

Even from the side, I could see his face had turned a pale shade of green. "I guess I did see something about it, now that you mention it."

"So, are you worried that it's a serial killer?" I asked him.

"I hope not," was all he said.

"I'm quite scared, which is why I want a fast car," Matilda said.

"I wouldn't worry yourself about it, dear. I'm sure you're perfectly safe. Don't you live in an aged care facility? I'm sure the nurses take good care of you."

We had now reached the quiet road. Matilda hit the gas, flinging me back in my seat. "Slow down!" the man said in horror.

"I have to see if this is its top speed," Matilda said, as cool as a cucumber. "Doesn't this road lead to a disused quarry?"

"Yes, err, yes," he stuttered.

We reached the quarry in no time, given the speed Matilda was going. She pulled off the road into the quarry and then pulled on the handbrake. The car did plenty of loops. I shut my eyes tightly and thought I might be sick. When the car finally did stop, the man unclipped his seatbelt, opened the door, and staggered behind a huge boulder.

"I think he's been sick," Matilda said with satisfaction. "He's so ageist and rude."

AN INSTANT CONFECTION

I clutched my stomach. "But do you think he's the murderer? Did you get any clues?"

"Not really, it's so hard," she said. "He would have had a reaction anyway because the victims were people in his old gang. Still, it's good to speak with him in person and get a general vibe from him."

"Matilda, here he comes now," I said urgently.

"Can we please go back now?" he said. His face had turned a horrible shade of pale yellow and deathly white.

"Yes, of course," Matilda said.

"Slowly. I don't feel well."

Matilda politely drove slowly all the way back. "I certainly like this car. It's come down to this one and a blue one that I also like. I will discuss it with Prudence and Horatio tonight. Would you have a card so I can call you if we choose this one?"

"Sure."

Matilda parked the car at the front of the steps. Scott held out his trembling hand for the key. "Wait here. I'll fetch my card for you."

However, Scott did not return. A fresh-faced young man came over and handed us Scott's card. He said Scott had suddenly taken ill.

CHAPTER 14

When we got to my front gate, I saw it was closed. I had almost forgotten about Billy. Matilda and I parked just off the road on the grass and we got out.

"That's a good idea. Eleanor's quite clever." I gestured to the large toolbox. "It looks quite heavy. I wonder how she got it here." I lifted up the lid and saw hay inside.

"Grab a large handful each," Matilda said. "We don't want to run out of hay."

I cast my gaze over the field. "I can't see Billy."

"He's probably hiding behind that black walnut tree," Matilda said. "Or maybe he's behind the house. Be on your guard, because Billy is quite cunning."

I had seen what Billy had done to the bishop. I grabbed a large handful of hay. It was with some trepidation that I slipped through the front gate with Matilda behind me.

"You hold the hay in front of you, and I'll hold the hay behind me, and when he arrives, we should be quite safe."

I wish I shared her confidence. I took off at a fast pace, but Matilda laid a restraining hand on my arm. "Don't run, because that will make Billy angry. You can walk quickly."

"I *was* walking quickly," I said. By the time we were halfway to the house, there was no sign of Billy. I was beginning to think he hadn't seen us yet, or maybe Eleanor hadn't taken him out of his own field yet, when all of a sudden I heard a horrible sound halfway between a bleat and a strangled grunt. I turned around to see Billy charging at us. I stuck the hay out in front of me, and so did Matilda.

Billy had his head lowered to charge, his long curved horns looking ominous, but when he saw the hay, he stopped in his tracks and then trotted over to us like a happy puppy. He grabbed the hay from me so hard I thought it would all leave my hand, so I held on for dear life. I started walking backward, holding the hay in front of me.

"You can't walk like that every day, Jane," Matilda told me. "I'm sure you're safe while you have hay. Just walk quickly and hold the hay out to the side. Whatever you do, keep a good grip on it."

I walked to the house as fast as I could. Every few steps, Billy grabbed another strand of hay from the bunch in my hand. It was all I could do to hold onto it. When we reached the door, I made to go in, but it was locked.

Billy was standing beside us on the porch.

"Eleanor!" I called out. I couldn't fish for the door keys in my purse because I needed one hand for the hay.

Eleanor opened the door a crack and said, "Not now!" She slammed the door.

"Excuse me?" I said. "We need to get inside in a hurry because Billy is here with us."

Eleanor opened the door, grabbed my wrist, and pulled me inside in one fluid motion. Then she repeated the process with Matilda before slamming the door behind us.

"What's going on?" Matilda asked her. "Have you completely taken leave of your senses?"

"It's Mr. Crumbles." Eleanor pointed to the cat

now sitting at the window, hissing and swishing his tail. I had never seen Mr. Crumbles so angry.

"He's taken a terrible dislike to Billy," Eleanor said. "That's why I locked the door. I didn't want him to get outside."

"Why doesn't he like him?" I said. "Is he like that with all the goats?"

"I don't think Mr. Crumbles has ever met the goats," Eleanor said. "Maybe he thinks Billy is a big dog or something. Or maybe a giant cat. Who knows? Mr. Crumbles does attack his reflection in mirrors though, so maybe he doesn't like other animals. Still, whatever the reason, we can't let him outside. Jane, we will have to keep all the upstairs windows shut."

"Fine," I said. "The sooner the police solve this murder, the better. Then all our lives can go back to normal. We won't have to carry hay from the gate to the house and be on our guard to make sure Mr. Crumbles doesn't escape and have an altercation with Billy." I walked over to the couch, threw myself on it, and dumped my purse next to me.

"Don't make yourself too comfortable," Eleanor said. "We have an appointment with Alan Dale."

"What, not today, surely?" I'd had a terrible and rather full day. My stomach was still a little queasy after Matilda's driving. "I was hoping this day had come to an end."

"You want to solve the murders, don't you?"

Matilda spoke up. "I texted Eleanor and told her what happened with Scott Simmons. He has my real name."

Eleanor nodded. "Then we can't go to Alan Dale and give him the same name. We have spoken to two bank robbers and one bank robber's wife, and all we have done so far is tell them we think there is a serial killer in town to judge their reactions."

I threw up my hands to the ceiling. "And how can that possibly help us? Surely, the murderer would have the same reaction as one of the gang who wasn't the murderer."

"I'm not sure I get your meaning," Matilda said.

"I mean, we have just spoken with Scott Simmons. When you said you thought there was a serial killer, he looked rather horrified. That is, he looked horrified at the mention of the murder of two of his former gang members. Even if he isn't the murderer, he would be horrified. And if he *is* the murderer, he would still look horrified. I don't see how that helps us."

"It's called reconnaissance," Matilda said. "You never know what you'll pick up from speaking with a suspect."

I shook my head. "But that's exactly my point. We haven't picked up a single thing yet. Not a single thing! We don't have a clue. The only thing we've gotten is tired. We are no further than we were this morning when we started all this."

Eleanor walked over and patted my shoulder. I looked at Mr. Crumbles. He was still hissing and swiping the window. "Don't be discouraged, Jane. Anyway, we might get some more information out of Alan Dale."

"I hope you're right," I said. "Didn't you say he sells cell phones?"

Eleanor shook her head. "I got the wrong person on Facebook. No, Alan Dale, the bank robber, is a stylist."

"A stylist?" I said. "Like, a hair stylist?"

I realized for the first time that Eleanor's hair looked like it had before it had the bizarre cut and color. "Eleanor, what did you do to your hair?" I asked her.

"It's a wig," she said. "I spent ages gluing it on, because I didn't want it to fly off."

I shrugged and repeated my question. "Is Alan Dale a hair stylist?"

"No, he works in a tanning salon attached to a styling salon."

I jumped to my feet. "There is no way I'm stripping down to my underwear and parading myself in front of a strange man!"

"He might not be all that strange, Jane," Eleanor said. "Granted, I know he was a bank robber, but he might be perfectly nice and rehabilitated now."

Matilda rolled her eyes. "I'm sure Jane means he is a man she doesn't know."

"That's right!" I said, clutching my purse to me. "No matter how keen you are to solve this murder, I am not going to take my clothes off and get sprayed."

Eleanor sighed long and hard. "All right then, I'll do it."

I was surprised. "You will?"

"Of course. That's why I glued on my wig. I've gone to a lot of trouble. I was hoping you would get a spray tan too, Jane, so both of us can question him, but it seems it's only going to be me." She hesitated and tapped her chin. "I know, I'll tell him that you want to see me sprayed, so you can decide whether or not to do it. That way, we can both chat with him."

I thought it over for a moment. "I suppose that would work." I considered I'd had a lucky escape.

Eleanor looked at her watch. "Oh, how time flies. We had better leave now, Jane. Matilda, make sure Mr. Crumbles doesn't get out. Actually, let's feed him in the kitchen now and lock him in there."

"Good idea," Matilda said. It took half a packet of treats and a lot of encouragement before Mr. Crumbles would stop hissing at Billy and go into the kitchen.

Eleanor and I slipped out the front door. "Quick, hay!" Eleanor said. She had placed a giant toolbox on the porch directly near the front door, so close that if Billy was already on the porch, we would be able to reach in and grab some hay before he attacked us.

Thankfully, Billy was no longer on the porch, and maybe that was why Mr. Crumbles had been willing to go to the kitchen.

We grabbed a handful of hay each and crept

down the front steps. "Don't run, because Billy doesn't like that," Eleanor warned me.

"Matilda has already told me that," I said. Once more, there was no sign of Billy until he suddenly appeared behind us. In fact, Eleanor heard him before I did and had already turned around. Billy seemed calmer, probably as he was used to Eleanor, given that she was the one who always fed him and cared for him.

Still, I was enormously relieved when I was on the other side of the gate and in the car. "I don't know how much more of this I can take," I said.

"Just think, if you wake up and you're scared there might be a murderer around the house," Eleanor said, "your mind will be at rest because Billy is patrolling the house."

"You know, you're right," I said. "I *will* sleep much better knowing Billy is outside."

The styling salon with the attached tanning salon wasn't too far from Rebecca's store. Eleanor announced herself at reception. She had given a false name, as usual.

"I booked Daisy Sue, my daughter here, as well, but she is too shy," Eleanor told the lady. "Would it be all right if Daisy Sue watches me get spray tanned so she can see there's nothing to worry about? Poor thing, she's never had a boyfriend, so she's shy, you know."

The woman looked me up and down. "Yes, of course, that will be all right. Cynthia, just change into these clothes and then pop down the corridor, first door on your right. There's a changing room in there. Daisy Sue, you can go with your mom."

I thanked her and walked down the corridor "Cynthia? Daisy Sue?" I whispered.

"You try to come with names," Eleanor whispered back. "But whatever you do, don't call me by my real name, because we could be dealing with a murderer."

A cold chill ran up my spine.

We walked into a room with a tent-like apparition in the middle. Over the far side, there was a sign on a door that said 'Changing Room'. "I'll be right back," Eleanor said.

A few seconds after she went into the changing room, the door opened, and a man stepped in. I knew from the Internet this was Alan Dale. "Aha, my next client," he said. "You were supposed to get changed."

"I'm just here with my mother, Cynthia," I said. "I was supposed to get a tan as well, but I was a bit scared, so the lady at reception said I could watch and see what happens."

He didn't seem the slightest bit interested in what had to say. "Oh yes, that's fine. I take it your mother is changing now?"

"Yes, she shouldn't be long."

Alan Dale ignored me and turned to some equipment. He muttered angrily to himself as he prepared it. I didn't get the impression he was altogether too confident with what he was doing.

Eleanor walked out in her underwear, a black lace thong, and a frilly bra that looked like an errant tutu. I gasped, and so did Alan Dale.

She greeted the man with a big smile. "I suppose I go in here?" She indicated the tent.

I would never have had the nerve to do what she was doing. "Yes, hold out your arms, and turn when I tell you to," he said. "How dark do you want it?"

"Does it take longer to make it dark?" she asked.

"Yes, I do a triple application."

"Do you have time to wait, Daisy Sue?"

"Yes, Mom, take all the time you like."

In fact, the whole procedure didn't take as long as I thought it would. One application looked good, but as he began the second, Eleanor turned a strange orange color. I thought I had better intervene. I walked over to them. "Mom, you're getting very dark. Do you think you should leave it at that?"

"I want to look dark," Eleanor said. To Alan Dale, she said, "Please ignore my daughter. She has a very nervous disposition, you see, which is why she wouldn't get a tan. She's terribly worried because murder victims have been found locally, and she's scared there's a murderer on the loose. It's made her far more nervous than usual."

"Oh yes, the dead bodies found under the floorboards of a house," he said. "I saw it on the news."

I thought that strange. His reaction seemed that of any regular person, not of someone who had known the victims personally.

"Yes, the news said they were bank robbers," I said, hoping to get some sort of reaction out of him.

Still, the deadpan face. "Yes, I read that." To Eleanor, he said, "Do you want me to continue? You'll go darker."

"Yes, I want to go extra dark," she said. "Just ignore my daughter. She's a hypochondriac, always imagining all sorts of illnesses. She is extra nervous now that the murderer hasn't been caught. She can't sleep at night. I hear her up and down the stairs at all hours of the morning. I hope they catch the murderer soon so I can have a good night's sleep."

"I sure hope they do." His tone was intense. After a short pause, he continued to spray Eleanor. Finally, he finished. "There, that's a nice, deep tan. Don't get any water on it or shower for at least six hours. And I do hope they told you to bring some old clothes, because it could stain your clothes. It's all written on this sheet of paper."

He handed Eleanor a piece of paper and then left the room. I went to say something to Eleanor, but she put her finger to her lips and hurried into the changing room. She soon emerged, fully clothed. "In the car," she said.

"What do you think?" I asked her as soon as we were in the car.

"When he said he hoped they caught the murderer, it seemed to me he was genuine. I didn't feel he was making that up, and he has no idea that the bodies were found under your house, Jane."

"Yes, I got the impression he was genuine as

well," I said. "It sounded as though he really did want the murderer caught."

"Then that narrows it down," Eleanor said, "unless the murderer isn't one of the gang members, but that seems highly unlikely."

Sadly, I had to agree. That meant that Matilda, Eleanor, and I would continue to be in danger until the murder was solved.

CHAPTER 15

The morning's newspaper provided some useful information. It mentioned the three remaining bank robbers, Martin Marks, Scott Simmons, and Alan Dale, as well as Martin Marks's wife, Daphne May. The article said that Scott Simmons had never been married, but it did mention Alan Dale's ex-wife, Donna, and mentioned that she owned an interior design store. It was there we were presently headed.

"Thank goodness the newspaper didn't give your name or address, Jane," Eleanor said.

"Obviously, the police didn't tell them," I said.

Both Matilda and Eleanor chuckled.

"What is it?" I asked them.

"There's always somebody who will talk to the

press," Eleanor said. "It's a good thing they didn't, in your case."

I agreed. "Yes, it would be awful to have journalists crawling all over the place. Should we go over our cover story once more?"

"I don't think we need to," Matilda said. "You have recently bought a home, and you need some decorating advice."

"Yes, it's hard with a mixture of our styles." And that was the truth. My idea of styling was at the opposite spectrum to the joint ideas of both Matilda and Eleanor. They liked bright, garish furnishings, and to say their style was eclectic was an understatement.

We had to park a few blocks away from Donna's store. "I hope she's working today," I said. "It would be awful to go to all this trouble and find a staff member there."

"We have to be prepared for every opportunity and turn every disadvantage to our own advantage," Matilda told me. "If there is a staff member present, then we can question that staff member about Donna Dale and her relationship to the gang. In fact, it might even be better. Always look on the bright side, Jane."

I sighed. "You're right."

When we first walked into the Retro Home Designs store, nobody was in sight. I was expecting a bright airy space with white walls, and fabric samples hanging from the walls, but instead this looked like an antiques store. Nineteenth-century spindle-backed wicker chairs sat beside heavy Jacobean and Edwardian dining settings. However, instead of the typical antique smell, the pleasant fragrance of lavender hung in the air. I suspected there might be one or more oil diffusers placed somewhere out of sight. The fragrance was too strong for potpourri.

A smiling woman emerged from a back room. She was shorter than the three of us, with shoulder-length blonde hair. She was dressed in a semi-casual manner, and when she approached, I saw she had flawless skin, and she didn't appear to be wearing much, if any, make-up. "Hello, can I help you ladies with anything in particular?"

Just then, the alarm over the doorbell tinkled, and two men in suits hurried in. "Donna Dale?" one asked her.

Donna took a step backward. "Who are you?"

"I'm Pete Smith, and this is my cameraman," the first man said. He continued to speak so quickly, I couldn't quite catch what he was saying, only that he was from a newspaper.

"I'm not speaking to the press," Donna snapped. "Please leave my store. You're trespassing."

The man ignored her. "And do you suspect your husband, Alan Dale? The police certainly do. Don't you think it's suspicious that your husband and his two accomplices got out of jail just before the bodies were found?"

"But the paper said one of those bodies has been there for years," Donna said. Her face had gone awfully pale. "Leave my store at once or I'll call the police."

"We're not doing anything illegal," the man said. "Do you suspect your husband is the murderer? Is that why you left him? And did you use the missing ten million dollars to fund this store?" The man's tone was overly belligerent.

Donna looked as though she was about to burst into tears. Matilda stepped between them. "Young man, leave this store right now."

He laughed. "What are you going to do about it?"

As quick as a flash, Matilda had him in a wrist lock and was escorting him out of the front door.

AN INSTANT CONFECTION

His cameraman traipsed behind, not giving any trouble. She gave the man a good push outside, and then Donna locked the door behind them and pulled down the curtains.

"Thank you. Thank you so much," she gasped. "I don't know what I would have done if you weren't here."

"Are you all right?" I asked her. It was clear that she *wasn't* all right, but I didn't know what else to say.

To my dismay, she burst into a flood of tears. "It's all been so horrible, so horrible."

"Can I make you a cup of tea?" Matilda asked her. "You look like you need a hot cup of tea with plenty of sugar."

Donna appeared hesitant and didn't speak for a moment. Finally, she said, "Oh yes, please, that would be lovely." She reached behind the curtain and flipped the sign to closed. "I'm sorry about all this."

"You have nothing to apologize for," I told her.

Donna led us to a little back room, in which was a small table just enough for four people as well as a little kitchenette. Matilda at once busied herself making a cup of hot tea for Donna.

"Please, all have a cup of tea or coffee, and I

have cookies in that canister over there." Donna nodded to a blue and white ceramic canister sitting next to a purple oil diffuser. That was the source of the delightful lavender fragrance, or at least one of the sources.

"I'm awfully embarrassed by all this," Donna said. "Did you understand what all that was about?"

I looked at Eleanor and Matilda for guidance.

Eleanor nodded. "I think so. I didn't realize it until the journalist spoke and mentioned Alan Dale. Wasn't he something to do with the bank robber gang? Two of the members were recently found buried under a house."

Donna dabbed her under her eyes with a tissue. "Yes, that's right. Alan Dale is my ex-husband. I didn't know he was a criminal, you see. He was my riding instructor, and I fell in love with him."

"A riding instructor!" I exclaimed. I wondered what he was doing tanning now, but I supposed he was trying to get any job he could.

"Yes, he was good with horses but not with people, as I found out to my detriment," she said. "He did dressage and he bought expensive Warmblood horses. I thought he had gained that money honestly. I divorced him when he was in prison. He was none too happy about it, but our marriage had been rocky for years. If he hadn't gone to prison, I would have divorced him, anyway." She sniffled again. "I had money when I married him, and I had this store before I married him. Now I have to be subjected to all those horrible questions about the missing millions."

Eleanor leaned over the table and patted her hand. "That must be horrible for you."

She nodded. "When Alan and the others were arrested, I lost all my friends."

Matilda placed a steaming cup of tea in front of her. "Well then, they weren't really friends if they abandoned you, were they?"

Donna gave a little nod. "I suppose so." She didn't sound convinced.

Matilda did a few trips back to the countertop. She placed a cup in front of each of us and then a plate of the cookies from the jar. "Eat up. You'll feel much better. My name is Suzanne, and this is my friend, Cathy. Over there is our young friend, Genevieve."

"Nice to meet you all. I'm Donna, but you probably already heard that."

I tried to keep the conversation going. "It must

be horrible for you, all this trouble from journalists, and I suppose, the police."

"The police!" she exclaimed. "They have been harassing me too."

Matilda's face showed mock surprise. "The police? Why would they bother you?"

"Well, because of the bodies," she said. "Two murder victims were found. One was murdered ten years ago, and the other was murdered recently. There were five members of the gang, and the bodies were two of the members. The three remaining members, my ex-husband, Alan, and the other two gang members were released from prison only recently, probably around the time of the second murder."

"I can understand why the police would question your ex-husband and the other two remaining gang members, but what does it have to do with you?" I said. "You divorced him years ago."

"They weren't accusing you, were they?" Matilda asked. "Surely, they can't suspect you?"

She shrugged. "I don't know. I always feel guilty when I see a police officer, I suppose, ever since I discovered Alan was a bank robber. They haven't suggested I get a lawyer or anything like that, but I've never really had much to do with the police. I mean, I did back when Alan was arrested—they questioned me a lot, and at the time, I'm sure they thought I was an accomplice."

"But they don't think that any more?" Eleanor asked her.

She shrugged again. "I don't think so, but you can never be sure, can you?" We all shrugged. She pushed on. "They asked me who had a grudge against the victims, Craig and Todd. They wanted to know if Martin, Scott, or Alan had a problem with Craig or Todd."

"I do hope you were able to give them some information, because that would get them off your back," Matilda said, rather cleverly, I thought.

Donna stirred her tea noisily, her spoon clinking against the tea cup. When she finally stopped, she said, "I told them Martin had a grudge against Craig."

"Was Craig the first victim?" I asked her.

She sniffled and nodded. "Yes, Craig was murdered some years ago."

"Why did Martin have a problem with Craig in particular?" Matilda asked her.

"Martin had a problem because his wife, Daphne May, was having an affair with Craig."

I was shocked but did my best to keep my expression neutral. "Were they having an affair for sure, or was it simply suspected?" I asked her.

"I think everybody knew," she said. "And of course, Todd didn't like Craig, because Craig..." Her voice trailed away.

Matilda leaned forward and patted her hand again. "That's all right. You don't have to tell us anything. Just talk if it makes you feel better. I'm glad we were at the right place at the right time, and we were able to get the journalist out of your store for you."

Donna shot Matilda a grateful look. "Did you read in the papers that there is a missing sum of ten million dollars?"

I continued to school my expression into a look of blankness, but Matilda nodded slightly. "I do think I recall hearing something like that." She sounded awfully vague.

"Todd always accused Craig of hiding that money. Todd thought Craig did it. There was no love lost between the two of them, that's for sure."

"Did the police seem close to knowing who murdered the men?" Matilda asked her. "Because once they solve the murders, you won't be bothered by the police or the journalists any longer."

Donna let out a long sigh. "You know, I don't think they have a clue, not as far as I could tell, but obviously they wouldn't let their thoughts be known to me." She appeared to be considering matters. It was a while before she spoke again. "Still, I got the impression they didn't really know. It was the questions they asked, that you see. They seem to be all over the place with no consistent train of thought. I figured their guess was as good as mine."

She shot us a half smile. "Now, is there anything in particular you wanted today? I'm happy to offer you a ten percent discount for all your help."

CHAPTER 16

*D*amon arrived unexpectedly to announce he was going to install the security cameras. An hour later, he told me he was coming back to finish installing the security cameras at three the following day.

"In the afternoon?" I said hopefully, even though I had a sinking feeling in the pit of my stomach. I was pleased Damon wanted to protect me. I just didn't know why he needed to protect me so early in the morning.

"No," he replied. "In the morning."

"You won't be able to see anything at three in the morning."

"Exactly. And no one will be able to see me. I

don't want anybody knowing there are security cameras outside your home."

"We could finish putting the cameras up now, couldn't we?" I really did not want to get up at three in the morning.

"I can't risk anyone seeing us. No one will see us at three in the morning." Damon was stubborn. I liked that in a man, which meant all I did to reply was sigh and nod. I could tell there was no talking him out of his three in the morning scheme. When a man decides he needs to do something to protect a woman, there is really little you can do to persuade him to act in a more reasonable manner. It was better to concede.

"I'm joking, Jane." His face broke into a wide smile. "I've finished installing the cameras, and I thought maybe we could have dinner."

I could feel my face grow hot. "Joking?" I exclaimed. I forced a smile. "Ha ha. I fell for it. Well, what about Chinese?"

Now it was Damon's turn to flush red. "I was hoping that I could cook for you, actually."

"You can cook?" This was news to me.

"I was hoping we could find that out together."

I poured myself a glass of wine and hoped

Matilda and Eleanor would stay at their friend's house for a good long time. There was something about sitting at the kitchen table, snacking on cheese, while watching a gorgeous man fuss about in the kitchen. I could get used to this life.

Damon tied on Matilda's apron, which was pink and covered with red roses, and winked at me. His shirt was a little too small, so the material pulled over his chest and arms. I didn't mind that one bit. He looked like Clark Kent.

"What are we having?" I asked, but only because I felt like a little silly sitting there in silence, staring.

"You'll see," he said, and then he winked.

I watched as Damon heated oil in a pan over medium heat, sighed as he added the garlic and cooked until the kitchen was filled with a gorgeous smell, swooned as he formed the meatballs in his strong hands, and shuddered as he cooked them for seven minutes. Who knew that a man performing the basic task of cooking could get me all hot under the collar, especially since I wasn't wearing a collar but a pair of pajamas Matilda had given to me last Christmas. They were awfully thick and covered with reindeer, and I'd kept them to wear while in the garden.

"What are you thinking about?" Damon said. He poured tagliatelle into a pot of boiling water.

"I should get changed," I replied.

"But you look so adorable," Damon said, and I could not tell if he was being sincere or not. "I have a pair of pajamas just like that."

"Don't tease me. I wasn't expecting you this evening."

"So you didn't wear this just for me?" There was a cheeky twinkle in Damon's eyes.

I decided not to dignify his remark with an answer. "Just stay right there, okay."

"Be quick. Dinner is almost ready."

I walked politely to my bedroom, and then I threw myself toward my cupboard like a mad woman Mr. Rochester would marry and then lock up in his attic.

I needed something cute to wear, but it couldn't be too cute, because then Damon would think I was flirting with him. It couldn't be *not* cute either, however, because I *did* want to flirt with Damon. I just didn't want him to know I was flirting or he would think I was a desperate spinster who should be at the rescue shelter adopting cats rather than eating his tagliatelle.

"Jane?"

"I'll be right there," I said, and I stuffed myself into a dress that I would need to hire a crane to get me out of later.

"I just thought I'd throw this old thing on," I said when I entered the kitchen.

"You look lovely," Damon said.

I hadn't realized just how puffy the skirt of the dress was when I had grabbed it out of my closet. "Well, I wanted to make an effort."

Damon laughed. "Have another glass of wine."

I smiled. Damon thought I was beautiful. I could tell not just by his words but by the way he looked at me, which is not a way a man had looked at me for a very long time indeed.

After dinner, Damon kissed me on the cheek. "Come and see the cameras."

He had installed seven cameras around the exterior of the house, and he showed me each one. We both had to feed Billy throughout the whole procedure.

"The cameras will alert you if they pick up anyone outside. I'll sleep a lot better knowing you are safe," Damon said.

"What about Billy?" I asked him when we were back inside. "Will he set it off the cameras?"

"I've changed the settings so they will only pick up somebody taller than a goat," Damon said. He downloaded the app on my phone and showed me how it all worked. He sat down next to me and wrapped an arm around my shoulders.

Were we a couple now? I could hardly tell. Still, things were moving along nicely.

CHAPTER 17

I was enjoying coffee by myself on a clear Sunday morning. Mr. Crumbles was sitting at my feet, purring loudly. Clearly, Billy wasn't in sight of the windows. Mr. Crumbles sure didn't like that goat.

I was on cloud nine after my lovely dinner the night before with Damon, and I had slept soundly.

I always appreciated the peace of the early mornings. It was time to get my head together in readiness for the day, and I welcomed the solitude.

It was not to last for long. Eleanor burst into the room, followed by Matilda. "Alan Dale, the tanning man, is going to attend a local church. I saw it on his Facebook timeline. We can all go there today to keep an eye on him."

I sighed and put my head in my hands. After an interval, I said, "Only one of the gang will be there?"

Eleanor shrugged. "As far as I know, but I don't believe people with a criminal record are allowed to associate with each other."

Matilda typically disagreed. "That differs from state to state. I think if they're no longer on parole, then they can associate with each other."

"But surely they *are* on parole," Eleanor said.

I rubbed my forehead, hoping I wasn't going to get another migraine. "Well, we will soon know when we get there, won't we!"

"Yes, and we will have to change our appearances," Eleanor said. "Alan Dale has seen the two of us, and if one of the other gang members is there, they will recognize Matilda."

An uneasy feeling settled in the pit of my stomach. "What type of disguise did you have in mind?" I asked her.

I looked at Eleanor, who was sporting a deep orange tan, as well as a green and red mullet.

"We will disguise ourselves to make ourselves look old," she said.

I bit back the obvious retort and instead

addressed Matilda. "And do you think it's a good idea?"

Matilda looked put out to have to agree with Eleanor, but agree she did. "I can't see what else we can do at this point," she said. "We simply don't have enough evidence."

"All right, then. What you intend to do with me?" I held up one hand for emphasis. "I'm not cutting or coloring my hair," I said in the firmest tone I could muster.

"No, that's all right. We're going to make you look old too, and we will make ourselves look feeble and weak."

"Couldn't I just go as I am?" I asked her.

My hopes were soon dashed when Matilda disagreed. "No, no, no. We are three ladies of definite ages, and if we are all seen together, that will be suspicious. Nobody will take notice of three ladies of our age. We will make you look at our age. And we will all bend over and walk slowly, as though we have no energy. Nobody will notice us. We'll be invisible, you'll see."

I had never worn a wig, and so I was unprepared for the lengthy process. First, Eleanor stuffed my hair none too gently into an overly tight hairnet and pinned it all down. "Now I have to use this gel to stick this wig cap to your head," she told me. She hesitated. "It's called gel, but it's actually strong glue."

I was horrified. "You're not serious, are you?"

She nodded.

"Does everybody glue wigs to their head?"

Eleanor shrugged. "We are not gluing the wig to your head, Jane. I will only glue around the front, and yes, that's the proper way to attach a wig cap unless you have a wig grip non slip headband of course, but we can't take the risk with that today."

She chatted on and on about the intricacies of wigs, and I zoned out. Finally, I said, "Okay, do whatever you like."

She applied the glue, and after an interval, poked at my head. "What are you doing?" I asked her, thinking perhaps I was better off not knowing.

"Just waiting for it to go tacky," she said.

Apparently, the glue was suitably tacky as Eleanor produced the most ghastly white wig I had ever seen and put it on my head. I was glad I wasn't sitting in front of a mirror. "That's not a very attractive wig," I commented.

Eleanor shot me a wide smile. "No, of course it

isn't. You're supposed to look like a semi-bald old lady."

"Great!" I rolled my eyes.

As soon as the wig was on my head to Eleanor's satisfaction and rather tightly at that, Eleanor produced a large box of make-up. "First, you should carefully put on some clothes," she said. "And be very careful putting anything over your head with that wig. Don't dislodge the band."

I had almost forgotten I had a tight band around my head, for the purpose of making sure the glue would stick nicely, according to Eleanor. I was glad the band wasn't going to stay there for too long.

Eleanor handed me the most horrible clothes I had ever seen. I wrinkled my nose. "What is that ghastly smell?"

"Mothballs, of course," Eleanor said brightly. "Some people think old ladies smell like mothballs. We will need to match their expectations."

Things were going from bad to worse. I pulled on the horrible old dress and thick, opaque stockings. "Can I look in the mirror yet?" I asked.

Eleanor chuckled. "No. You need to wait until I do your make-up so you can have the full effect."

I wasn't sure I wanted the full effect, but I was

already committed to the process. I sat there in silence while Eleanor applied my make-up. "We're giving you some lovely contouring to make your cheeks look sunken and give you lots of wrinkles and deep furrows," she said happily. "This is only a rush job, mind you."

"I'm glad you're not getting carried away, Eleanor," Matilda said, her tone approving.

"What do you mean by carried away?" I asked her.

"Eleanor is fantastic at make-up." Matilda frowned as she gave her sister a compliment. "She does the best fake wounds of anybody I've ever seen. Why, she does the most wonderful gunshot entry wounds of anybody in the business."

I narrowed my eyes. "And what business is that?"

Matilda waved one hand through the air. "It's just a figure of speech. You know, anybody who is good at make-up."

Eleanor stood back to admire her work. "Excellent."

"Can I look in a mirror now?"

"Yes, but I want you to practice walking first." Eleanor handed me a walking stick. As soon as I took it, she snatched it back from me. "I'll demonstrate. You need to walk like this. The heavy shoes will help."

The heavy shoes were, in fact, pinching my toes horribly, but when I remarked on that to Eleanor, she said that would help me to stay in character. I did several laps of the living room before the sisters were satisfied with the way I walked.

"Now you can look in a mirror," Eleanor said.

I made to walk up the stairs, but Eleanor put a restraining hand on my arm. "Stay in character from now on, Jane. Hobble up the stairs and take a long time getting there."

I carefully walked up the first few stairs and then looked over my shoulder. The sisters were looking at me. Eleanor gave me the thumbs up sign in encouragement. I walked a few more steps quite carefully and hunched over and then looked back. They were still looking at me. I sighed and slowly made my way to my bedroom.

When I looked in the mirror, it was all I could do not to let out a bloodcurdling scream. I looked absolutely nothing like myself. I did indeed look like an unhealthy and quite elderly woman who had seen better days. I edged closer to the mirror, part of me not wanting to look at all but part of me fascinated by the clever make-up Eleanor had done.

I barged out of my bedroom door and hurried to the top of the stairs, before remembering I had to stay in character. I hobbled down the stairs slowly.

"What do you think?" Eleanor asked me.

"I look absolutely ghastly!" I said.

A wide smile broke out on her face.

"How long will it take you two to get ready?" I asked them.

"Probably an hour," Eleanor said.

I gasped. "A whole hour? Do I have to stay in these clothes and look like this for an hour?"

They both nodded. "You'll need an hour to practice," Eleanor said.

I was none too pleased. The hour seemed to drag on for ages, and in fact dragged on for almost two hours.

When Eleanor and Matilda appeared, I was shocked. They both looked like I did, both wearing similar types of wigs. Both had deep furrows under their eyes, and their complexions were sallow and sickly. Eleanor's ghastly orange tan had been replaced by a pale, sickly, white complexion. The sisters were also stooped over and clutching walking sticks.

"Well then, Jane, let's go to church," Eleanor said in overly happy tones.

That's when it occurred to me. "We have to get past Billy!"

Eleanor bit her lip. "All right then, we won't stay in character until we get to the car."

With the three of us holding hay, we made our way through the field quite safely. "Billy is used to being fed when he sees someone near the house now," Eleanor said. "If the murderer does come here again, Billy will be in an even angrier frame of mind when he doesn't get fed." She chuckled.

I simply shook my head and jumped in my car.

We were a little late arriving at church. Everybody was already seated. I figured that was just as well as we didn't have to mingle with any crowds. I followed the sisters' lead, hunched over, and walked slowly toward the church with my walking stick.

We took our seat on pews in the back section of the church. The people were already singing a hymn. Eleanor covered her face with her hymnbook and said to me, "There's Alan Dale over there near the front."

"Which one is he?" Matilda asked. Eleanor pointed him out to her.

"Can you see any other gang members?" I whispered. We all looked around the room.

"No, but I can see Detective Collins and Detective Wright," Matilda said.

"They're here?" I was shocked. Did that mean they thought Alan Dale was the murderer? Or were they simply keeping an eye on all of the suspects?

We sat through the whole church service. The minister told plenty of jokes, and everyone laughed heartily. However, he spoke for a very long time. When he began, "And now, to conclude my sermon," my spirits lifted.

After he concluded his sermon, he said, "And now, after the closing hymn, church members and visitors alike are invited to have fellowship one with another in the side room here." He pointed over his left shoulder. "Everybody is welcome."

While everyone was singing the closing hymn, Eleanor said, "I'm going to speak with Alan Dale again."

"But he'll recognize you," I said.

Eleanor chuckled. "No, he won't. You can come with me, and you'll see. Matilda, you keep an eye on the detectives."

"Yes, I was going to suggest that," Matilda said.

The second the hymn was over, people hurried to the next room. It took the three of us a while to get there, considering we had to walk very slowly.

As soon as we got in the door, Matilda broke off in the direction of the detectives, while I followed Eleanor straight to a table filled with cookies.

"Let's grab something to eat before we go and speak to Alan," she said. I selected a graham cracker with cheese, while Eleanor selected a small chocolate cupcake. As luck would have it, Alan was at a nearby table making himself some coffee. He was only inches from us. Eleanor at once addressed him. "Excellent service today, as usual."

He offered her a tight-lipped smile.

"I haven't seen you here before, I don't think," she continued. "I'm Susan Chaffey."

"Nice to meet you. I'm Alan Dale."

"I was a little concerned that we didn't have prayer requests today," she said. "I wanted to pray to keep us all safe from the murderer."

Alan's face drained of color. "Oh yes, the murderer," he said. "Maybe we could put in a request for that next week."

"Is this your first time here at church?"

He shook his head. "No, I've been coming here for a while now."

Eleanor chuckled. "I'm so sorry. My eyes aren't what they used to be, and I'm rather hard of hearing too. Would you please put in the prayer request for next week? Please ask that the murderer is found before he murders anybody else. I can never hear what the minister says as he speaks so softly."

Alan looked as though he wanted to get away from Eleanor quickly. "Yes, I will."

He made to turn away, but she tapped his arm. "None of us are safe in our own homes, are we, not with the murderer on the loose?"

Alan shook his head and then scurried away, snatching up a chocolate chip cookie on his exit.

Eleanor at once spoke to a young man who had now come up to pour coffee. "Excellent service today, wasn't it?"

"Yes, it was good," he said.

"Have I seen you here before?"

He nodded. "My wife and I come every week."

Eleanor chuckled. "Oh, I'm a little forgetful." She turned back to me when he left. "Jane, take my arm and guide me to those slices of apple pie on the back of the table."

I did just that.

"I wanted it to look as though I spoke to various people, in case the police were suspicious," she said, "but of course they wouldn't be. I told you Alan wouldn't recognize me."

"You were right," I said. "Even *I* hardly recognize you."

"We'll have to wait around until some people leave so that we don't stand out."

I nodded. I cast a glance over at the detectives. Matilda was quite close to them, sipping from a Styrofoam cup of coffee. They appeared oblivious to her presence.

I couldn't believe it was going so well. Still, the wig was hot, tight, and uncomfortable, and I didn't like wearing the heavy shoes. I was sure I had terrible blisters on my toes and heels.

It seemed like an age before anybody left, and then I elbowed Eleanor. She signaled to me to walk out of the door. We waited in the car for a full five minutes before Matilda came. "Drive off, Jane," she said.

I did. "Did you overhear anything interesting?" I asked her.

"Only that they were here for Alan Dale. I could tell they are absolutely mystified. They don't seem to have a clue who did it. They also mentioned Scott Simmons and Martin Marks."

"In what context?" I asked her.

"In the context that they don't seem to have a clue who did it. What about you two? I saw you speaking to Alan Dale, Eleanor."

Eleanor repeated the conversation and then concluded, "But I thought he looked quite frightened when I mentioned the murderer. What did you think, Jane?"

"I thought he looked frightened, too."

Matilda nodded. "Maybe he was frightened because the detectives were in the church. Obviously, they would have questioned him by now, and he knew they were there to keep an eye on him."

I disagreed. "You know, I don't think that was it. Eleanor asked him to put in a prayer request that the murderer would be found before he murdered anybody else, and he did seem genuinely scared."

"Scared of the murderer?" Matilda asked.

"Yes." I was dismayed that the police didn't seem to have one suspect in particular. There were three surviving members of the gang. I hoped the police would have made more progress by now.

CHAPTER 18

"Ouch!" I shrieked as Eleanor tugged on my hair.

"Sorry. It needs more alcohol." She dabbed some more alcohol on my hair. "I think I used too much glue."

"You think?" Before I could say any more, Eleanor made a sound of triumph and pulled the wig cap off my head. "Ouch!" I shrieked again. I rubbed a patch on my head. "Did you pull out a chunk of hair with it?"

Eleanor put the wig cap behind her back. "Maybe one or two hairs might have come out with it."

I stood up and put my hands on my hips. "I'm never wearing a wig again."

"You won't have to wear one this afternoon," Matilda said.

I gingerly rubbed the sore spots on my head. My whole scalp felt tender. "What do you mean by *this afternoon*? I wanted to take a nap or at least watch television or do something relaxing."

"How can you be relaxed with only Billy to protect you?" Matilda said.

I was wary. "What did you have in mind for this afternoon? We have questioned all the suspects, surely."

Matilda readily agreed. "Yes, there's nothing else we can do there. No, we need to fill in the gaps."

I was puzzled. "What gaps?"

"The whole changing hands of this property doesn't make sense," Matilda said.

"It makes sense to me," I protested. "Martin Marks's parents owned it, then Martin inherited it and sold it to the petting zoo people, who sold it to the Amish people, David and Arleta Habegger, and they sold it to my sister and her husband."

"But that doesn't explain why the first body ended up in the tunnel."

"It doesn't explain why *either* body ended up in the tunnel," I pointed out.

Matilda waved one finger at me. "No Jane, you don't get my point. I'm talking about Craig Williams, the skeleton, the first victim. He was a member of the bank robbery gang, but at the time Martin sold this house, there was no tunnel there. How did any gang members know about the tunnel?"

I had to admit she was right. "You know, that never occurred to me."

All of a sudden, there was a terrible commotion. Mr. Crumbles was flinging himself at the living room window. All his hair was standing on end, and he was enraged.

Eleanor hurried over to close the curtains. "Oh dear. I had no idea Mr. Crumbles had such a bad case of goatophobia."

"There's no such thing as goatophobia. You made that word up, Eleanor!" Matilda said crossly.

Eleanor pointed to the cat. "Try telling Mr. Crumbles that."

I rubbed my forehead a little too hard and then winced. Those sore spots were going to last a long time. "So, we're going to question the petting zoo people. What exactly are we going to ask them?"

"This will be much easier," Eleanor said. "We

don't have to wear a disguise or pretend we are other people. We can tell them the truth."

"And what exactly are we going to ask them?" I persisted.

Matilda shrugged. "We're just going to get the timeline right and see if they kept in touch with Martin Marks. Who knows what information they will have?"

I stood up. "All right then, let me put on my usual clothes and get this make-up off my face, and then let's go there now." I crossed my arms over my chest. "But this is absolutely the last place I am going to today. No matter what happens, you must give me your word that when I come home today, I will not have to leave the house again."

Matilda and Eleanor looked none too happy, but they both agreed that I would not have to leave the house after the next fact-finding expedition.

It took us a while to entice Mr. Crumbles to the kitchen, locking him in with treats, and then we walked to the car while holding out bunches of hay. Billy walked alongside us, snatching strands of hay from our hands. I was certain I could see in his big yellow eyes that he half wished there wasn't hay so he could butt us with his long, curved horns.

It was with relief that I once more shut the

gate behind me, leaving a now angry and hay-less Billy standing inside the gate, looking daggers at us.

"So, have these petting zoo people retired or what?" I asked.

Matilda shook her head. "On the contrary, they still have a petting zoo and a restaurant."

"I wonder why they sold this place then? Are they now closer to town?"

Eleanor consulted her map. "No, not at all."

With Eleanor navigating, I soon found my way to the petting zoo. "Oh, now I can see why they sold. This is a much bigger place than my house," I said. There was extensive parking out the back and down the side of a huge brick building. It seemed to be a substantial restaurant, and in fact, *Petting Zoo Family Restaurant* was blazoned across the front in a large blocky red typeface.

"Let's have lunch first and look at the lay of the land," Eleanor said.

"Honestly, Eleanor, these aren't suspects."

"How do you know that, Jane?" Eleanor said. "Everyone's a suspect. Besides, I'm starving," she added lamely.

"I'm hungry too," I said. "What with the pain in my head for hours from that dreadful wig, I hadn't realized I hadn't eaten. We forgot to have lunch."

"Then let's have lunch now," Matilda said, resignation in her tone.

We walked inside the building where the big sign announced that we could pat the animals for a dollar and buy a packet of alfalfa pellets for a little more.

"That would be a good idea," Eleanor said. "Jane, you could have a petting zoo at your place and charge a dollar for entry."

"No way!" I said, a little more firmly than I intended.

Eleanor's face fell. The restaurant was crowded, but Matilda soon spotted a vacant table and guided us to it. We took some time looking at the menus. "Everything looks good," I said. "I can't decide. What are you two having?"

"I think I'll have the Grilled Chicken Breast with onion, lettuce, and tomato," Eleanor said.

"I'm going to order the Slow Roasted Roast Beef in Gravy with mashed potatoes and French fries." Matilda jabbed her hand on the menu. "It says mashed potato *or* fries, but I'll ask for both."

I bit my lip and studied the menu a bit longer. "I'm going to order the Homemade Tuna Salad with egg, cheese, as well as fries. At least I won't feel so guilty if I eat tomatoes and greens. I'm absolutely starving."

A waitress appeared by our table and took our order. "Would you like drinks while you're waiting?" she concluded.

We all ordered coffee. When the waitress left, I asked them, "When are we going to speak with the owners?"

"After lunch," Matilda said.

"And we'll pay the dollar and go to the petting zoo first," Eleanor added.

Matilda nodded.

"Why would we do that first?" I asked them.

"Surveillance," Eleanor said. "It's a good idea to take in your surroundings at the first opportunity."

"Okay." I was relieved when the coffee came. It helped my hunger a little, but I was surprised when the meals were quickly delivered given the place was so crowded. Maybe we had arrived at just the right time when everybody else had been served.

"Oh, this is so good," I said after I had consumed a few mouthfuls.

Matilda set down her fork for a moment. "We should come here more often."

I agreed with her. "Sure. The food is good and very reasonably priced, and it's not too far from us. Plus, there are lovely views over the fields."

After we ate some AP Cake for dessert, Eleanor suggested we should have some ice cream, but both Matilda and I said we didn't think we could fit in another morsel. "We'll get some ice cream after we speak with the owners," I told Eleanor. She seemed satisfied with my response.

We walked out to the petting zoo and paid the attendant a dollar each.

"Look, there are alpacas," Eleanor said. "Jane, didn't you want an alpaca?"

"No, I certainly never wanted an alpaca," I told her, "as cute as they are."

Eleanor planted her palm on her forehead. "Silly me! You wanted a horse."

I was taken aback. "You're right! I *do* want a horse. How could I have forgotten that? There's been so much going on."

Matilda pointed to the goats. "There are goats, but they don't look like our goats, Eleanor."

"No, they don't have horns," Eleanor said. "I suppose that makes it safer for children to pat them."

I cast my eyes around my surroundings. The

animals were all clearly well cared for. There were cows in a field by themselves, and then one field held both sheep and alpacas. The goats were in a field by themselves, but all around and wandering freely were turkeys, geese, and peacocks.

Matilda tapped my arm and pointed to a peacock, which was fanning his tail and strutting in circles in front of a peahen that didn't appear the least bit interested in him.

After an interval, we walked back to the attendant. "Are Sean and Chloe Barden here?" Matilda asked. "We'd like to have a word with them."

The attendant narrowed her eyes. "Do you have a complaint? Is there anything I can help you with?"

I shook my head. "My name's Jane Delight. Sean and Chloe used to own my house. I just wanted some information from them about my house. It has a few irregularities they could help me with."

The attendant's face relaxed. "Yes, of course." She summoned over a waitress and explained we wanted to speak with the owners. The waitress indicated we should follow her to an office.

The office was attached to the side of what

appeared to be the Barden's house. It jutted out like a sore thumb and was made of glass and metal, whereas the house was homey and brick. A man looking completely overwhelmed was sitting in small, cluttered room hunched over a keyboard, tapping away on the keys. A huge stack of paperwork sat directly to his right. There was no sign of a woman. He looked up, surprised to see us.

The waitress addressed him. "This lady owns a house you used to own." With that, she left.

I shot him my widest smile. "I'm Jane Delight, and these are my housemates, Matilda and Eleanor Entwistle. I own the house that has a tunnel under it."

A look of recognition flashed over his face. He stood and walked over to shake our hands.

"You might have heard that two bodies were discovered under my house recently."

He nodded vigorously. "Yes, the news didn't mention the address, but two detectives came to question us."

"They did? Yes, well, that's what we're here about. We wanted to understand the timeline," I told him.

"The timeline?" he repeated.

I nodded. "As you know, there are two houses on the farm, my house with five acres and the adjoining house on the bigger farm." He nodded. I continued. "My sister, Rebecca Yoder, and her husband, Ephraim, live in the main house, and they sold the house on five acres to me. That's the one with the tunnel under it."

Matilda interrupted me. "Rebecca and Ephraim bought it from an Amish couple, David and Arleta Habegger. Jane's sister was under the misapprehension that the Amish couple had built the house, but apparently they bought it from you?"

Sean nodded. "That's right. Lovely couple. They were a bit dismayed that they'd have to remove all the electricity, though." He chuckled.

Matilda pushed on. "But didn't you buy it from Martin Marks?"

"Yes, that's right. We had no idea he was an infamous bank robber at the time. Or rather he was a bank robber, but no one knew that, least of all us, when we bought it from him."

A lady walked into the room. "I thought I heard voices," she said. Sean introduced her as his wife, Chloe, and told her why we were there.

"And we have just gone into your petting zoo

and had some lovely lunch in your restaurant," Matilda told her. "We decided we will come back here on a regular basis since your food is so good."

Chloe beamed from ear to ear. "It's lovely to hear such nice feedback."

"Now, we were trying to get the timeline right," I said. "You bought the property from Martin Marks?"

They both nodded.

"And you converted the house to a café, and you build a tunnel under it?"

Chloe chuckled. "Yes, it might seem strange to you now that it's converted back to a house again."

"The big room with a tunnel under it," I said. "What did you use that for?"

"We made that room look like a pirate ship," Chloe said. "The space underneath the floor was a pirate's grotto, and we owned the field next door that the tunnel came out into."

Her husband took over the explanation. "When we sold everything, we sold your house on five acres and the farm next door to the Amish couple, but we sold the field where the tunnel comes out to a botanist. He was a professor."

"Somebody owns that land?" I was surprised. "I thought it was woods."

Chloe shook her head. "I know the man who bought it wanted it to remain woodland. He was a scientist, you see," she added as if that explained everything.

Eleanor spoke for the first time. "The first victim was Craig Williams, who as you would no doubt be aware, was in the Johnson Gang with Martin Marks. He was found under the floorboards of where your pirate ship would have once been. Did Martin Marks know there was a tunnel there? Did he ever visit you after you opened the petting zoo?"

"Oh yes," Sean said. "When we bought the place from him, we told him of our plans. He seemed interested, and he asked us to let him know when it was built. So we did."

"And did he come out to take a look?" I asked them.

"Yes, as a matter of fact, he did. He even made an offer to buy it back, but we refused, of course. We had just spent a considerable sum renovating it all. He had an extensive look through the tunnels and everything."

"I see," Eleanor said.

"We're probably of no help to you," Chloe added.

"No, you've been a wonderful help," Matilda said. "Thanks so much for the information. And now we must get Eleanor some ice cream."

Eleanor clasped her hands with glee.

While Eleanor was selecting a flavor of ice cream, I turned to Matilda. "This is all making my head spin. What conclusions have you drawn?"

Matilda came straight to the point. "Martin Marks knew there was a tunnel and a grotto. That would have been an ideal place for them to hide the bank robbery money."

"And a dead body or two," I added.

CHAPTER 19

I awoke just before the sun the following morning and yawned and stretched. I had spent another peaceful night. Maybe the intruder from the other day didn't want to come back at night or wanted to wait until things quieted down. I expected whoever it was thought the police would be keeping a close eye on the place.

I was awake a little earlier than usual, so I tiptoed downstairs to brew the coffee.

As the sun dawned, casting pink and gold rays through the lace curtains on the kitchen window, I heard the sound of a buggy.

"Billy!" I exclaimed. I opened the door, grabbed a handful of hay, and sprinted to the buggy. It was Wanda. "*Hiya*, Wanda. Have you seen a goat?"

Wanda looked surprised. "A goat? *Nee*, are you missing a goat?"

I shook my head. "No, Billy is Eleanor's dangerous goat. We have let him loose in this field so he can attack any intruders. You didn't see him when you opened the gate?"

"*Nee*, maybe he was scared of the horse." Wanda's big black Saddlebred snorted and pawed the ground.

"Maybe. Oh, there he is now." Billy peeped around the corner of the building. He didn't run over for hay. That was good—maybe he *was* scared of the horse, after all.

"Is it safe for me to get out of the buggy and tie up my horse?" Wanda asked me.

"It seems so," I said. I kept an eye on Billy until we reached the front door. "You go inside, and I'll put the hay back in the toolbox."

Wanda did as I asked. Eleanor and Matilda were waiting at the bottom of the stairs. "We heard your phone beeping, Jane," Matilda said. "We knew somebody was here." She waved the phone at me.

"My phone!" I said. "I left it in my bedroom."

"How did you get in here past Billy?" Eleanor asked Wanda.

"Billy seems to be afraid of Wanda's buggy horse," I said. "He was peeking around the side of the house but didn't come over to us."

"And you didn't see him when you opened and shut the gate?"

Wanda shook her head. "*Nee*, I didn't see any goat, apart from the ones in the field, that is."

"Come and have breakfast with us," Matilda said. "I'm quite partial to *kaffi* soup now. I can make you some."

Wanda hurried ahead of us into the kitchen. I told her to sit down and wouldn't accept her offer of help. I poured all of us some coffee, while Eleanor made Wanda some coffee soup.

"And would you like sausages and bacon? Maybe scrapple?"

"*Denki*," Wanda said. "I suppose you're wondering why I'm here."

"What?" Matilda said in mock horror. "You mean you're not here for my brilliant *kaffi* soup?"

Wanda chuckled. "Actually, Waneta has some news."

I was all ears. "What sort of news?"

"Apparently, everyone thought the men were killed with axes."

"They did have axes protruding from their heads," Eleanor said. "Do you mean there was another method used as well?"

Wanda nodded slowly. "Waneta said the toxicology reports have come back, and the second victim had hydrocone bitartrate in his system."

"What's that?" I asked. "I've never heard of it."

"I have," Matilda said. "Isn't it a type of opiate, used for severe pain?"

"Indeed it is," Wanda said, "at least according to Waneta."

I was perplexed. "But was he taking it by prescription, or was it given to him to kill him?"

Wanda finished her mouthful of coffee-soaked bread before speaking. "Waneta said the victim had very high levels in his system, too high to be taking it for health reasons. What's more, he had alcohol in his system, and it's highly dangerous to take hydrocone bitartrate at the same time as alcohol."

I turned my coffee cup around while I was thinking. "So then, does that mean somebody tried to kill him with a combination of hydrocone bitartrate and alcohol, and when that didn't work, gave up and thought they might do him in with an ax? A more direct method, so to speak."

Wanda shrugged. "Waneta didn't say. She only said that he had very high levels of hydrocone bitartrate as well as alcohol in his system, and it is contraindicated for alcohol."

"That's most useful, most useful indeed," Eleanor said.

Matilda agreed. "From memory, hydrocone bitartrate in large doses can cause dizziness."

"Yes, that's right," Wanda said. "Waneta said something like that."

"I'll just check on Jane's phone," Matilda said. Before long, she added. "The side effects are indeed dizziness, as well as nausea, vomiting, lightheadedness, and drowsiness, and in large doses it causes severe drowsiness, difficulty waking up, mood changes, and difficulty breathing."

Eleanor picked up Mr. Crumbles and set him on her lap. "So, it seems that the murderer gave him a drink laced with alcohol to kill him."

Wanda set down her spoon with a thump. "Oh, silly me! That was the most important thing Waneta wanted me to tell you all. It wasn't a fatal dose."

"You mean he didn't have enough hydrocone bitartrate in his system to kill him?" I asked her.

"*Jah*, that's right."

"Not even even with the addition of the alcohol?"

Wanda nodded. "*Jah*. There wasn't enough to kill him, just enough to make him very sick."

"You know what this means?" Matilda asked. We all looked at her and she quickly added, "Or what it could mean."

I thought it over. "This could mean that killer wanted to embed an ax in Todd's head but wanted to render him weak enough to do it. I didn't get a good look at the victim, only that he did seem to be a large burly man. This leads me to believe that the murderer couldn't match him for strength and so wanted to weaken him first with hydrocone bitartrate and alcohol. That way, the murderer could deliver the killing blow."

"Yes, that certainly sounds right to me," Eleanor said.

"And how would anybody get this hydrocone bitartrate?" I asked them.

"Waneta said it's prescribed for moderate to severe pain," Wanda said.

"But one of the bank robbers could scarcely go

and get a prescription for this and then murder someone with it," I said. "It would be far too obvious."

"But the murderer wasn't expecting the body to be found so soon," Matilda pointed out.

I didn't like it, and I said so. "I don't think anybody would take such a risk. Maybe the murderer has a relative who has been prescribed hydrocone bitartrate."

Eleanor agreed with me. "Yes, I like your idea, Jane."

We all fell silent while we ate the last of the scrapple.

After we finished breakfast, Wanda said she had to get back. I accompanied her to the front door and let her out. Mr. Crumbles was calm, which meant Billy wasn't near the house. I walked Wanda to her buggy and then kept an eye out for Billy as she opened and then shut the front gate.

When Wanda was safely on her way home, I walked back to the kitchen. Matilda and Eleanor had their heads together, speaking. They looked up when I walked into the room. "This is a huge clue," Matilda said. "The murderer had to gain access to hydrocone bitartrate."

"That's why it's such a big clue," Eleanor added.

Matilda ignored her. "Why did the murderer give the victim hydrocone bitartrate and alcohol, which clearly was designed to weaken but not kill him? This is why: the murderer wanted an ax in the victim's head."

"Exactly like the first victim," I said. "It seems the murderer wanted both victims to die by means of an ax."

"And if we knew why, then we would be well on our way to knowing who the murderer was," Matilda said.

I poured myself another cup of coffee. When I had finished it and was fully caffeinated, something occurred to me. "What if there were two murderers?"

Matilda and Eleanor's jaws dropped open. "*Two* murderers?" Matilda asked.

"Whatever do you mean?" Eleanor asked. "Where are you going with this, Jane?"

"I don't know that I'm going anywhere in particular," I admitted, "but think about it. We've been assuming there was one murderer because the victims were in the same place and they were killed by the same method."

"A reasonable assumption," Matilda said, "but now you think differently, Jane?"

I nodded slowly. "I initially thought it was the one murderer, but now that this hydrocone bitartrate substance mixed with alcohol has been found in the second victim, it makes me wonder if it was done to weaken him so the murderer could attack him with the ax. The very fact that the body was in the same place as the first victim…"

Eleanor interrupted me. "That could have simply been because it was a good place to hide a body."

I agreed with her. "Yes, quite possibly. But what if it wasn't?"

"Please don't be so mysterious," Matilda said. "Come to the point and tell us what you're thinking, even if you think it sounds silly."

"What if the second victim had murdered the first victim, and the second victim was killed as an act of revenge?"

Matilda nodded vigorously. "So you think victim two, Todd Johnson, murdered Craig Williams? And another murderer killed Todd Johnson in revenge for killing Craig Williams?"

I nodded. "That's exactly what I'm thinking. It

might be a stretch, but I believe it's certainly a possibility."

Matilda and Eleanor looked at each other and nodded. "It's certainly a possibility," Matilda said. "So if we investigate along these lines, we have to find somebody who liked Craig Williams enough to revenge his death, and it would also have to be somebody who had access to hydrocone bitartrate."

"And somebody who wasn't physically strong enough to overpower Todd Johnson and kill him with an ax," Eleanor added.

"Then who could that be?" I asked. "The other members of the gang don't look terribly strong. I mean, Scott Simmons and Alan Dale don't look terribly strong. However, Martin Marks does look as though he could have subdued Todd Johnson."

"And he was aware of the old pirate grotto under your floorboards, Jane," Matilda said.

Eleanor added, "And he was limping, and clutching his leg at intervals. What if he has a prescription for hydrocone bitartrate?"

I nodded at Eleanor. "But if Todd Johnson did kill Craig Williams, why would he go back to the scene of his crime, and get murdered there himself?"

"Yes, we have to figure that one out too," Matilda said. "And why would Martin Marks use a drug he himself was prescribed on a murder victim? That is far too obvious."

While Matilda and Eleanor continued to discuss the matter, I was in despair. I felt we were further away from solving this murder than when we had started.

CHAPTER 20

I was sitting home alone—that is, if you don't count Mr. Crumbles. The little cat had worked himself up into quite a state, running from window to window to look for any sign of Billy.

For the first time in ages, I was alone with my thoughts. I considered the hydrocone bitartrate. Had the murderer simply made a mistake and had gotten the dose wrong? No, the more I thought about it, the more I decided that the murderer did want to embed an ax in the victim's head. The key was that the second victim was murdered in exactly the same way as the first victim.

At first, I had thought it was the same murderer, but now I didn't think that at all. The hydrocone bitartrate with alcohol could have been designed to weaken the man so he could be killed with the ax.

The murderer had to lure him somehow to the pirate grove under my floorboards. I had a suspect in mind, but I needed more information.

I walked up and down my living room for several minutes and then decided I should go back to Donna Dale's store. I did need some new curtains. The ones at the far end of the living room were old and yellowed lace and were patchy. I expect they had been there for years. To provide privacy and as a temporary measure, Matilda and Eleanor had covered the windows with bright, multi-colored blankets they had bought during one of their visits to India many years ago. The sequins reflected the light and caught my eye every time I walked into the room. As a migraine sufferer, this wasn't a good thing.

I grabbed my tape measure and measured the windows. Normally, I would have bought ready-made curtains, but I needed another excuse to visit Donna Dale. If my hunch proved correct, then it would be worth spending the extra money.

As soon as this murder was solved, I would be

able to walk freely outside my own home and not have to worry about Billy's horns coming for me.

Matilda and Eleanor were at their weekly Zumba class, and they usually went to a café afterward with the other participants. I left them a note just in case I was delayed. I tried to lure Mr. Crumbles into the kitchen with treats, but today he was too recalcitrant. I had no hope of catching him. It took me some time to get out of the door without letting him out of the house.

As soon as I was outside, I reached into the toolbox as fast as I could and grabbed a handful of hay. I was so tired of doing this. I couldn't wait for the police to apprehend the murderer, so I could then walk outside and sit on my porch, drinking coffee or meadow tea and enjoying myself.

I was halfway to the gate when an uneasy feeling crept over me. I spun around, the hay held out. Billy had suddenly appeared behind me. He fixed me with his big yellow eyes.

"Nice Billy, nice Billy," I said in soothing tones, although the goat looked anything but nice. I held out the hay. Billy hurried over and snatched some hay from my hand. I was getting better at hanging onto the hay now, although I had red marks all over my palm.

I held the hay out to my side and walked as quickly as I could to the gate, with Billy trotting beside me. At least, this time he appeared less threatening, and he hadn't lowered his head at me in a threatening manner for a full five hours.

I slid through the gate and then threw the rest of the hay on the ground for Billy. He didn't even raise his head to glare at me. "I can't wait until you're back in the field with your goat friends," I told him.

I drove straight to Donna Dale's store.

Once more, when I let myself in, there was nobody in sight, but she presently emerged from the back room. Her face lit up when she saw me. "Oh, hello. Genevieve, isn't it?"

She looked genuinely pleased to see me.

"Yes, I've brought some measurements for curtains," I said. "As we said the other day, I'm renovating my house. I'm only at the beginning of the renovating, so I have to watch the budget."

"That's very wise," she said. "Renovations typically take twice as long as you think and cost twice as much as you think."

I laughed. "I'm afraid I'm finding that out the hard way." I produced the piece of paper with the measurements and showed her. "These are the measurements of the window, and I have a photo on my phone."

I pulled my phone from my purse and showed her photos of my house interior. While she was looking at the photos, I watched her face for any sign of recognition, but her expression remained impassive. Either she was a very good actor, or she hadn't been the intruder in my house. I was beginning to think I was right in my suspicions of the identity of the murderer.

"What fabric do you have in mind?" she asked. "What colors do you have in there now? Apart from the ones I saw on your phone, of course."

I couldn't help chuckling. "Well, my friends, um, Suzanne and Cathy, decided to help me decorate. They used bright reds and purples and all sorts of strange things. While I'm grateful for the help, that isn't my taste at all."

"What is your taste?"

I shrugged. "Cozy, really. I like looking at pictures of the English countryside with pretty pink and white tea cups or even fall tones. I'd say my style is cozy."

She nodded. "Come and have a look at my pattern book."

In the next room, she showed me a sample

featuring a delightful pattern of roses on a cream background, but with a contemporary twist, and then suggested I look through her pattern book.

"Did you see anything in there that you liked?" she asked after a few minutes.

"I did," I said. "I didn't realize I'd have so much choice."

"I have more samples. Come and see."

Donna led me around the corner to a part of the store I hadn't seen before. "This is more a cottage style here, but it's kind of a combination of cottage style and Hamptons style," she said. She pointed to the curtain sample on the fake window behind her.

I clapped my hands with delight. "Oh yes, this looks delightful. This is my style, for sure. I'd love curtains exactly like that." The fabric was delightful, but I wondered how I would bring the conversation around to the murder.

"Come over to the desk and I'll do some prices for you."

Donna indicated I should sit at a desk opposite her, and she pulled out a notepad and a calculator.

"Have the police been back?" I asked her.

She looked up at me and smiled. "No, thank

goodness. It's such a relief that they're leaving me alone."

"Has that awful journalist been back?"

Her expression clouded. "The journalists have been leaving me alone, too."

"Maybe the police are closer to discovering the murderer," I said.

She set down her pen and let out a long sigh. "I certainly hope so. I feel as though I can't get on with my life until they do."

I plastered what I hoped was an absent look on my face and looked at the ceiling. "I wonder who it was," I said absently.

To my dismay, she didn't take the bait. I looked back at her, and she was punching keys on her calculator. Finally, she gave me a figure for the finished curtains. "How does that sound to you?" she asked me.

"Yes, that would be fine," I said. "How long would it take?"

"It's usually fourteen working days," she said. "Would that suit you?"

"Yes, that's fine. Do I pay now?"

"We usually ask for a deposit, but you can pay now if you like. It's up to you."

I said I would pay now. I told her I would come and collect the curtains as soon as they were ready.

"Would you prefer me to call or text?"

"Either would be okay with me," I said. I leaned forward and said in a conspiratorial tone, "I hope you don't think I'm strange, but I absolutely love watching murder mysteries on TV. Ever since I realized your ex-husband was involved in the gang, I've been trying to figure out who the murderer was."

I thought she would be angry or at least a little annoyed, but instead she looked intrigued. "Who do you think it is?"

"The newspapers assumed it was the one murderer, somebody who might strike again, but then I wondered—what if there were two separate murderers?"

Her jaw dropped open. "I hadn't even thought of that."

I sat silently and waited for her to say more. After a moment or so, she did. "But why would the bodies be in the same place and murdered in exactly the same way, if it wasn't the same murderer?"

I tapped my chin and tried to not look too intense. "This might be a strange idea, but it occurred to me that the second victim had actually murdered the first victim, and then the second victim was murdered in revenge."

She appeared to be processing the information. "So you think Todd murdered Craig, and then another person, a second murderer, murdered Todd in revenge?"

I nodded. "Exactly. And if it was a revenge killing, then maybe that's why the second murderer killed Todd in exactly the same way Craig was murdered, and in the same place too—because it was a revenge killing."

"I suppose that's possible. I'm glad I've left all that behind me." Donna appeared to have lost interest. She pushed my receipt across the desk to me. "I'll let you know as soon as your curtains are ready."

I thanked her. I stood up and walked toward the front door. Somebody ducked back behind the front door and hurried away.

I turned back to Donna. "Isn't that the hairdresser, Daphne May, who just left?"

Donna appeared surprised. "Oh, do you know her?"

I nodded. "She does the hair of a friend of mine."

"Yes, we're having lunch today. Maybe she thought I was busy and didn't want to bother me."

I smiled and said goodbye. As I left the shop, there was no sign of Daphne May.

There was only one reason she would run away from me. She had overheard what I said, and she knew I had figured out she was the killer.

CHAPTER 21

On my way home, I imagined I was being followed. Or maybe it wasn't my imagination. I didn't actually see a car following me—it was a horrible sensation. Maybe I was simply unnerved because I thought Daphne May had overheard what I said.

Or had she? Maybe she had seen me there and recognized me from the other day. No, that didn't make sense. She wouldn't have recognized me from the back of my head. She must have overheard what I was saying.

I had left a long voicemail message for Damon, telling him that I suspected Daphne May was the murderer. I explained my reasons.

When I got home, I parked at the front gate and looked behind me. No one had followed me, and there were no other cars in sight.

I breathed a sigh of relief and reached into the toolbox for a handful of hay. With my purse in one hand and hay in the other, I walked toward my house.

All of a sudden, Billy leaped out in front of me. "You half scared me to death!" I squealed.

I immediately held out the hay to him. He came forward and latched his teeth onto it, pulling as hard as he could.

I continued the rest of the way to my house in that manner. Just before I reached the porch, I looked over my shoulder. There was still not a car in sight. I breathed another long sigh of relief. Maybe Daphne May hadn't figured out I was onto her after all, or maybe she figured I had called the police and told them of my suspicions.

As I opened the door, a terrible sound made me jump. I realized it was Mr. Crumbles trying to get through the window to attack Billy.

My nerves certainly were on edge. I checked my phone again to make sure hadn't missed a call from Damon. I hadn't. I had, however, missed a text from Matilda who said she and Eleanor would be home presently.

I walked into the kitchen and made myself a cup of meadow tea. I carried it into the living room and put it on the table just as there was a loud sound at the door.

The front door flew open. There, standing in the doorway, was Daphne May.

I broke into a cold sweat. My heart beat out of my chest. I struggled to breathe. "What are you doing here?" I squeaked.

She shut the door behind her just in time to prevent Mr. Crumbles from running outside.

"How did you get here?"

"Through the tunnel, of course."

"But what about the gate?"

"I have a key," was all she said.

She took a step toward me. I took a step backward. "Are you the murderer?" I asked.

"Of Todd Johnson? Yes." She added a few rude words.

"But why?" I asked.

"Craig Williams and I were lovers. I was going to leave Martin for him, but Todd murdered him. He thought Craig was hiding some money."

"Was he?"

"Yes, as a matter of fact, he was. I assumed Craig told Todd where it was before Todd killed him, because Todd suddenly came into money at that point."

"Did your husband know this?" I asked her.

She made a horrible sound at the back of her throat, halfway between horse neighing and a pig snorting. "Of course not! That fool doesn't know anything! He loves his dog more than he loves me! Anyway, I have to stay married to him for a while now so the cops won't be suspicious of me."

"Detective McCloud knows it was you," I said. "He's on his way to arrest you now."

"Do I look like I believe that?" She cackled. "No, I recognized you when you came in to get your hair done."

I was puzzled. "But how?"

"I've had to keep an eye on this house, of course, ever since I murdered Todd," she said. "I murdered him just before you bought this house. You ruined all my plans! I knew that Amish couple owned the house, so I thought I was perfectly safe murdering him there, and I didn't see the house advertised for sale."

"That's because the Amish person I bought it from is my sister," I told her.

"I knew what you and your two old friends looked like. When you came into the salon, I figured you were being amateur sleuths. Fancy yourselves as Miss Marple, do you? Maybe Jessica Fletcher?" She held her stomach and burst into raucous laughter.

"Did you poison Todd first?"

She nodded and then showed me her flexed biceps on one arm. "I might be strong, but I was no match for Todd. I told him I'd discovered my husband was hiding a large sum of money under a big rock in the grotto. I said I wasn't strong enough to move the rock and offered to split the money with him if he could retrieve it. The fool believed me. I insisted we have a glass of champagne before I showed it to him. I wanted to weaken him so I could tell him I was going to kill him in revenge for Craig."

"And that's why you murdered Todd in exactly the same way that Craig was murdered."

"Yes, that's exactly right," she said smugly.

I was beginning to think she was quite unhinged. I eyed the distance to the wall where the weapons had been hanging and then remembered that Eleanor and Matilda had hidden them before

Detective Collins and Detective Wright had come the other day.

I heard my phone beeping on the table where I had thrown it and looked at it. It was a security notification that a person had been detected outside my house. Well, there was certainly something wrong with the system's timing!

Daphne May pulled out an ax that had been tucked in the back of her jeans. I saw she was wearing gloves. "I'm going to put you down under the floorboards with the others," she said.

"But they're not there now." I know it was a silly thing to say, but it was the first thing that came into my head.

She looked somewhat perplexed. "That will throw the police off the track. They'll think it's a serial killer."

"But I actually have already told the police that I knew it was you. I've told the police," I repeated.

"I don't believe you, and there's no evidence at all," she said. "I'm just a simple hair stylist. I was trying to frame my husband, but that didn't seem to work."

"How were you trying to frame him?" I wanted to keep her talking until Matilda and Eleanor came home.

"Because he has a prescription for hydrocone bitartrate for his bad leg. That's why I used it on Todd. I also made an anonymous call to the police that the gang members still had ten million dollars. I was hoping the police would suspect Martin."

"It is strange that they don't," I said. "But then again, you have access to it as well, so they are just as likely to suspect you."

"They haven't taken me in for questioning, so I really don't think they suspect me," she said. "And do you know how hard it is to make a murder charge stick? They have to have a lot more than just suspicions."

Daphne May brandished the ax and lunged for me just as the door opened. She swung around to see Matilda standing in the door. She made a dash for Matilda, but Matilda and Eleanor both jumped inside, Matilda flinging the door wide open.

Billy ran into the house.

Both Eleanor and Matilda were holding hay, so Billy shot me an evil look. He also shot Daphne May an evil look, and she was closer to him than I was.

He lowered his head and charged. Daphne May got out of his way just in time, and his horns slammed into the couch. While this was all happening, I somehow had the presence of mind to run to Matilda, who gave me half her handful of hay.

Daphne May was certainly agile. She picked herself up and sprinted for the door, but Billy lowered his head again for another charge. Mr. Crumbles had fallen asleep and was lying on the top of the dresser. When he saw Billy run past, he became enraged. He jumped onto the goat's back, digging in his claws as the goat picked up speed.

Daphne May ran out of the house, screaming, with Billy right behind her, Mr. Crumbles still on his back.

Matilda, Eleanor, and I got out of the door just in time to see Billy's horns connect with Daphne May's bottom. She was airborne for a second. She went into a bush headfirst, her legs pointing to the sky. Billy stood there, pawing the ground and snorting at her.

I suddenly noticed Damon's car. I hadn't even seen him drive through into the gate. He ran over to me. "Jane, are you all right?" He pulled me into a deep hug.

I returned his hug, not caring who was watching. "Daphne May was going to murder me with an ax," I said. "She murdered Todd because

AN INSTANT CONFECTION

he had murdered Craig for the missing money. She and Craig were having an affair."

I turned around to see that Daphne May had extricated herself from the bush. She had sprinted to a nearby tree and climbed the lower part. She was only a few feet from the ground. Billy was standing on his hind legs, with his front legs resting on the tree doing his best to reach her. She was mere inches from his horns.

Damon chuckled. "She will be safe there until the detectives come," he said.

"And it wasn't Mr. Crumbles who saved Jane this time," Matilda said.

Eleanor disagreed. "Of course it was Mr. Crumbles! He jumped on Billy's back and made Billy go faster." She was clutching Mr. Crumbles to her. He was eyeing Billy and hissing.

"But Mr. Crumbles didn't *technically* save her," Matilda said. "Billy would have saved her, anyway."

"But Billy saved her in a better way because Mr. Crumbles was there! You have to admit that Mr. Crumbles has had a hand—rather, a paw—in saving Jane every time somebody has tried to murder her!"

"Some things never change," Damon

whispered in my ear as he guided me inside, hopefully to make me a nice cup of hot tea and give me a cake filled with carbohydrates and fat and other things not good for me. It was just what I needed.

CHAPTER 22

I had decided to make a picnic for Damon. Mr. Crumbles kept falling asleep in the vintage basket, however, which meant I had to pack the wheelbarrow with my treats. I'd made old-fashioned lemonade—the secret is to make a sugar syrup so that the sugar doesn't float around the bottom—and grilled corn on the cob. Matilda and Eleanor helped me too.

"The way to a man's stomach," Eleanor told me, "is through his heart."

"You mean the way to a man's heart is through his stomach," Matilda corrected her.

"Is it?" Eleanor looked thoughtful while Matilda and I used a fork to mash the avocados. I wanted to make a chunky guacamole too.

It was hard to keep Matilda away from the Reese's Peanut Butter Fluff. We used cream cheese for structure and instant vanilla pudding for thickness. Of course, we used peanut butter too. My favorite part, aside from eating the fluff, was folding the little Reese's candies into the mix. It was a fair effort doing so in front of Matilda, who kept trying to eat the candies.

"This is not enough food for a young man," Eleanor said, placing her hands on her hips. "Where's the potato salad? Where's the pasta? Where's the white bean and broccolini salad?"

"Damon doesn't want broccolini," Matilda scolded, her mouth full of peanut butter and chocolate. "He wants barbecue wings."

"Does he?" Eleanor rubbed her chin. "No, he's too thin."

"Thin?" I tried not to sound defensive. Damon was the perfect specimen of a man: broad shouldered, with arms that would put any athlete to shame. I thought about my own flabby arms and shuddered. Still, he liked me for me, fat rolls and all.

"I don't believe he eats enough," Eleanor replied. "Trust a bachelor to live off frozen food."

"Damon has a wonderful diet," I said, not knowing if this was true.

Eleanor snorted rudely. "If his bottom gets any flatter, some conspiracy theorist will think it is the earth."

"His bottom is perfect!"

"Jane, you must not look at his bottom," Matilda scolded me. "It isn't proper."

I frowned. "But Eleanor did?"

"Eleanor is an elderly spinster, which means she can do whatever she likes. That is the advantage of age, young Jane. Nobody is offended by anything we say or do."

"But I'm offended."

"You are also over seasoning the potato salad."

"We should go on this picnic too," Eleanor said. She clapped her hands as if she just had a bright idea.

"No," I said. "What? No. Absolutely not."

"We need to make sure that man eats," Matilda agreed.

Eleanor nodded. "We need to fatten him up."

Matilda agreed. "Absolutely."

"Absolutely not," I corrected her. "You two are not coming on my romantic picnic with my almost boyfriend. He'd think I was the strangest person in the world."

"Then how will we know if Damon has eaten a good amount of food?"

"You won't," I said.

Eleanor looked hopeful. "A food diary?"

"No! Have you both gone mad?"

A minute later I was holding a quill and a pot of ink, a roll of parchment tucked under one arm. "Let me get this straight," I said. "You want me to record every bite of food Damon McCloud eats on our picnic with this quill?"

Matilda and Eleanor nodded.

"This quill is bigger than my head," I said, because the feather truly was bigger than my head, and the hottest shade of hot pink you'd ever seen.

"It's pink. It's very feminine," Eleanor said.

I sighed. "We had better pack the wheelbarrow before Damon gets here. It may take us some time. We've made enough food to feed an entire army."

Damon arrived just after we'd finished packing. I couldn't find Mr. Crumbles anywhere, not even in the picnic basket, and I wanted to kick myself for not bribing him out of the basket with his favorite treats earlier.

If I had done that, I would not be strolling next

to Damon as he drove the wheelbarrow down to the pond. Instead, I'd be giggling as I swung a picnic basket off my arms, as delightful and beautiful and charming as someone out of *Little House On The Prairie*.

Thankfully, Matilda had insisted I wear a dress she'd worn in the eighties, one with huge sleeves, so I looked like a shepherdess frolicking through a sun-kissed field. I knew Damon liked the dress too. He kept glancing at me and grinning, the wheelbarrow jolting over the uneven ground.

"Did you notice how I didn't ask why you were carrying a quill, ink pot, and roll of parchment?" Damon said.

"I did notice that."

"I didn't ask because I assumed an explanation would be forthcoming."

"I don't want to tell you."

"Why?"

"Because it's embarrassing."

"Even better."

"Eleanor believes you need to eat more, and she wants me to keep a food diary."

"Of?"

"Of everything you eat." Not only were my cheeks burning, but my ears were burning too.

"Of everything I eat?" Damon laughed. "Matilda and Eleanor really are a dream."

"I think the word you are looking for is a *nightmare*," I grumbled.

"Why don't we invite them, Jane? It would make so much more sense than you writing down what I eat on a roll of parchment." Damon chuckled. "After all, Mr. Crumbles has already decided to join us."

I looked over my shoulder, expecting to see the little cat padding behind us down the field. "He has?"

"Look!" Damon nodded to the wheelbarrow, where a furry little tail was sticking up from beneath the picnic rug. "I wonder if he was worried I wasn't eating enough too."

"Oh, Mr. Crumbles believes someone in this world isn't getting enough to eat," I said. "Himself."

Damon laughed.

"You should see the way he follows me around, meowing. It's as if he'd never eaten a day in his life. I think Mr. Crumbles believes we're starving him."

Damon stopped pushing the wheelbarrow, linked arms with me, and guided me back along the field to the house. Soon we were back at the wheelbarrow again, but this time we had with us Matilda and Eleanor. The one advantage of collecting them was that I got to leave the quill, ink pot, and parchment at home.

"We don't want to impose," Matilda said.

"Yes, we do," Eleanor replied.

Soon the five of us—including Mr. Crumbles—were sprawled out on the picnic blanket I'd inherited from my grandmother. Not one of us got to try the fluff, because Matilda had eaten the entire bowl and then practically licked the bowl clean. Thankfully, no one wanted me to keep a food diary for Matilda, because she had devoured half of the picnic after eating all the fluff. I couldn't keep up! But she was happy, and that is all that counts.

Mr. Crumbles was happy too. He sat by the pond, attempting to catch a duck. Of course, he wasn't really trying to catch a duck. If one swam close to him, he sprang away from the water and ran over to Damon, who he had clearly decided was his protector.

"So," Eleanor said, "are you two in a courtship?"

"A courtship?" Damon laughed. "That's a very sweet way of putting it, Eleanor."

I blushed, and then I blushed some more. Damon looked at me and winked.

"You two do make a handsome couple," Matilda said. "Was it love at first sight?"

Damon's eyes twinkled. "You could say we had an instant connection." He popped a chocolate cupcake in his mouth.

"I think you mean," Matilda replied, "an instant confection."

We all laughed, except for Mr. Crumbles, who took the opportunity to eat the tuna casserole while we were all distracted.

As I sat there by the water, the breeze gentle lapping in my hair, I thought about how hard things can seem sometimes, how dark the world can feel. If only I had realized years ago that the best remedy for the dark shadow that could sometimes cross my heart was a picnic in the fresh air with two lovely ladies, one very fine man, and one cheeky little cat named Mr. Crumbles.

I knew then that everything always turns out all right in the end.

AMISH RECIPE

AP CAKE

INGREDIENTS

2 1/2 cups all-purpose flour
1 cup brown sugar
1 cup butter
2 cups buttermilk (Add 1 teaspoon lemon juice to milk, stir, set aside for 10 minutes.)
1 egg, beaten
1 teaspoon salt

1/2 teaspoon baking soda
1 teaspoon baking powder
1 teaspoon vanilla extract

METHOD

Mix flour, sugar, salt, vanilla extract, baking powder, and baking soda.

Combine the butter and flour to create crumbs. Set aside 2 cups.

Mix the milk and crumb mixture. Divide between 2 x 9 inch pie pans.

Pour in flour, sugar, salt, vanilla extract, baking powder, and baking soda mixture.

Spread 1 cup of crumbs over each cake.

Bake for 45 minutes in a 350 degree F preheated oven.

Serve either warm or cooled.

AMISH RECIPE

AMISH PEANUT BUTTER PIE

1 x 9 inch pie crust

PUDDING INGREDIENTS

3 cups milk
1/2 cup cornstarch
1 tsp. salt
1 tsp. vanilla

AMISH RECIPE

3 egg yolks

3 Tbsp. butter

1 cup sugar

1/4 cup smooth peanut butter

CRUMB MIXTURE INGREDIENTS

2 cups powdered sugar

1 cup crunchy peanut butter

3 cups whipped cream or whipped topping

METHOD

Mix crumbs mixture until mixture forms crumbs.

Place some crumbs in the bottom of the pie crust. Set aside the rest of the crumbs.

Scald milk over medium heat.

Combine egg yolks, sugar, vanilla, and salt and pour into scalded milk.

Heat and stir until thick.

Allow to cool.

When cold, add 3 cups of home whipped cream or whipped topping.

Place pudding into the baked pie crust.
Spread whipped cream or whipped topping.
Top with remaining crumbs and serve.

NEWS!

I am excited to announce that this series is being produced in audio by Findaway Publishing (not to be confused with Findaway Voices) for release in 2021!

Ruth

ABOUT RUTH HARTZLER

USA Today Best-selling author Ruth Hartzler spends her days writing, walking her dog, and thinking of ways to murder somebody. That's because Ruth writes mysteries and thrillers.

She is best known for her archeological adventures, for which she relies upon her former career as a college professor of ancient languages and Biblical history.

www.ruthhartzler.com

Made in the USA
Coppell, TX
16 August 2021